ESCAPE FROM SHUDDER MANSION

NIGHT of the LIVING DUMMY

NIGHT of the LIVING DUMMY 2

NIGHT of the LIVING DUMMY 3

STAY OUT of the BASEMENT

The HAUNTED MASK

ONE DAY at HORRORLAND

The CURSE of the MUMMY'S TOMB

The WEREWOLF of FEVER SWAMP

The SCARECROW WALKS at MIDNIGHT

RETURN of the MUMMY

REVENGE of the LAWN GNOMES

VAMPIRE BREATH

PLEASE DON'T FEED the VAMPIRE

The GHOST NEXT DOOR

ATTACK of the GRAVEYARD GHOULS

Scholastic Children's Books
An imprint of Scholastic Ltd
Euston House, 24 Eversholt Street, London, NW1 1DB, UK
Registered office: Westfield Road, Southam, Warwickshire, CV47 0RA
SCHOLASTIC, GOOSEBUMPS, GOOSEBUMPS HORRORLAND
and associated logos are trademarks and/or registered trademarks of Scholastic
Inc.

First Published in the US by Scholastic Inc, 2018
First published in the UK by Scholastic Ltd, 2019

Copyright © Scholastic Inc, 2018

ISBN 978 1407 19585 8

Goosebumps books created by Parachute Press, Inc.

A CIP catalogue record for this book
is available from the British Library.

Printed by CPI Group (UK) Ltd, Croydon, CR0 4YY
Papers used by Scholastic Children's Books are made
from wood grown in sustainable forests.

3 5 7 9 10 8 6 4 2

www.scholastic.co.uk

Goosebumps SlappyWorld

ESCAPE FROM SHUDDER MANSION

R.L. STINE

SCHOLASTIC

SLAPPY HERE, EVERYONE.

Welcome to My World.

Yes, it's *SlappyWorld*—you're only *screaming* in it! Hahaha.

You know, being a living evil dummy is a tough job—but *someone's* got to do it. And who does it better than me? Ha.

I only wish I had longer arms. Then I could pat myself on the back.

Hey, I'm going to a party tonight. Know why I get invited to so many parties? Because I'm a SCREAM! Hahahaha.

But don't call me dummy, dummy. My IQ is so high, you have to climb a ladder to read it! Ha.

I don't want to brag. I have faults just like anyone else. Know my biggest fault? I'm TOO AWESOME! Hahahaha.

Now, here's a story that will haunt you. That's because it's about a haunted house.

Riley Shiner knows it's a house of monsters and evil spirits. But he and his twin sister, Scarlet, decide to spend the night there anyway. Just

1

think of all the scary things that could happen to them.

Actually, you don't have to *think* about them. Because I'm going to tell them all to you in GRUESOME detail. Hahaha.

I call this story *Escape from Shudder Mansion*. But the title is a lie—*because there IS no escape!* Hahaha.

It's just one more terrifying tale from *SlappyWorld*.

Every time I see the huge, old mansion, my mouth goes dry, and I feel a chill tighten the back of my neck. When I step into the yard, I can feel the temperature drop at least ten degrees.

I guess that's because the ancient trees are so tall, they block out most of the sunlight. But I think the cold is coming from the house, seeping out through the cracked windows and crooked doors.

With its black slate roof and high stone towers, the house rises above the treetops and casts a deep shadow, no matter the time of day. The house is nearly hidden by the trees that grow at the garden's border at the edge of the sidewalk. You have to step far into the yard until its dark walls and blackened windows come into view.

By that time, it's *too late*. Too late to escape its ghostly coldness . . . too late to escape the evil as it curls around you and freezes you in its icy grip.

Okay, okay.

I know I got a little carried away there. You don't know me yet. If you knew me, you would know that sometimes I get excited and go a little overboard.

I am Riley Shiner. I'm twelve. My twin sister, Scarlet, knows me best. Scarlet says I'm just like her guitar. Sometimes the strings get wound too tight and make a shrill sound.

She says I'm just like those strings. Wound too tight.

LOL, right? I can't argue with Scarlet. And I can't get angry at her because she makes me laugh. Scarlet is funny.

People expect a lot from you when you're twins. For one thing, they expect you to look alike. Well . . . Scarlet and I don't.

She is tall and thin and has wavy red hair and blue eyes. I'm about three inches shorter and a little chubby, and my hair and eyes are dark brown.

When people meet us for the first time, they don't think we're twins. They don't even think we're brother and sister! "Actually, we're *identical* twins," Scarlet tells people. That always cracks us both up. Most people just get confused.

"You have to listen to me, Riley," Scarlet says. "Because I'm twelve minutes older than you."

I don't know if she means that or not. Does she really think she can boss me around because she's the big sister?

Anyway, it was after school and she was leading the way through the trees in back of Shudder Mansion. Yes. Shudder Mansion. The name of the house says it all. It was maybe the *last place* I wanted to be.

I stepped in front of her to block her path. "Scarlet, why do we have to go this way? You know the stories about this place."

"It's a shortcut," she said.

"And we're in a hurry because . . . ?"

"I'm late for my Wednesday guitar lesson," she said.

"But today is Thursday!" I protested.

"That means I'm *really* late!"

I told you. She's funny.

She pushed me out of her way and started walking a zigzag path through the trees. I gazed at the back of the house. The stone walls were cracked—long cracks that looked like lightning bolts. Two back windows were boarded up, the glass missing.

I felt another chill.

"Scarlet, this isn't going to save us any time," I said.

"Not if you keep stopping," she said. She narrowed her blue eyes at me. "You don't really believe the stories about this mansion—do you?"

"Maybe," I said. The word came out in a squeak. "Look at this place." I motioned with one hand. "It *has* to be evil."

She shook her head. "Seriously. You have *got* to stop playing that video game."

You have to understand. Shudder Mansion is so scary and so famous, there is an awesome, best-selling video game about it. The game is called *Escape from Shudder Mansion*. And to tell the truth, I'm kind of obsessed with it.

I mean, how many games take place right in your neighborhood? The game starts two blocks from my house!

I've played it so much, I know every room, every twist and turn of the dark halls. It's about these evil spirits that are trapped in the house. They want revenge for their fate on anyone who ventures into the house.

Sometimes the spirits take the form of humans. Sometimes they become monsters. You never know what's around the corner or behind a door.

As you play, you accumulate weapons. The idea is you have to destroy each evil spirit before it can kill you—or you will become one of them, trapped in Shudder Mansion forever.

I've made it to the fourth level. It wasn't easy. I had a lot of scary moments and close calls and

I died a lot. The fifth level has a scary monster that I haven't been able to destroy no matter what I try.

Scarlet keeps telling me it's just a game. But . . . where did the idea for the game come from? It came from the real Shudder Mansion. And what if the game makers were telling the truth? What if they didn't make the story up?

A lot of horror movies are based on true stories, right?

So I think you can see why I didn't want to take a shortcut through the back lawn. Even if Scarlet was late for her guitar lesson.

"Come on, Riley. Hurry," she said. "Stop looking at the house."

Standing in a small clearing of trees, I couldn't take my eyes off it. I squinted into the shadowy, flickering light—and thought I saw something. Something like smoke, narrow and black. I watched it float out of one of the broken windows.

I gasped. "Scarlet—look—"

But she was far ahead of me, making her way through the trees.

Unable to breathe, or move, I watched the black shadow grow larger as it whirled away from the mansion. Blacker than the other shadows, like a cloud of ink, it curled low to the ground, taking the shape of a snake, slithering, folding in on itself, raising a fanged, triangle-shaped head.

And then I remembered this black, snaky creature—from the video game!

I'd seen it. I'd seen it—and I'd *never* defeated it.

And it's coming for me, I realized.

Silently, it slid and curled over the grass, in a straight line now, a straight line toward me. This black serpent shadow.

My whole body went cold. As it slithered closer, I could feel its evil washing around me.

I could feel it. I could feel it. The whole yard turning dark now.

I opened my mouth in a scream—spun around—and started to run.

2

I stumbled over a clump of tall weeds. My backpack flew over my head as I tumbled to the ground. I landed hard. The breath shot out of me with a loud *whoosh*, and pain spread over my chest.

I wanted to scramble to my feet, but I couldn't breathe. I rolled onto my back, choking, gasping for air.

I raised my head and saw the black shadow coming closer. I watched it rise up like a tall ocean wave. It spread out and rose higher, higher. Then it swept over me.

I lay there helpless, still unable to breathe, smothered in its coldness now, covered in blackness. And inside the shadow, deep inside, I saw the glow, the blazing glow of red eyes.

Red eyes flaming inside a monstrous face, a face twisted and distorted, with lips like fat worms, lips that opened to reveal two sets of pointed gray teeth.

I stared helplessly at the glowing red eyes as the shadow creature spread its blackness over me. I shivered and shook. I struggled to toss it off.

But it clung to me. Wrapped itself tightly around my shoulders. And started to shake me hard.

It shook me. Shook me so hard my teeth rattled. I struggled to see it in the total darkness.

And then the shadow lifted. I blinked as the trees above me came into focus. Rays of yellow sunlight flashed and flickered in the leaves.

I gazed up. It was Scarlet, shaking me by the shoulders—not the monster inside the black cloud. She had both hands on my shoulders. She was on her knees, leaning over me, shaking me.

Where was the evil shadow?

Scarlet finally let go and climbed to her feet. "What's wrong, Riley?" she demanded. "Why are you on the ground?"

I raised my head. "A shadow—" I murmured.

"Get up. What are you doing down there?" She lowered a hand to pull me to my feet.

But I didn't take her hand. Instead, I stared at the creature beside me in the grass. A cat. A green-eyed black cat.

"Whoa!" I uttered a cry and jumped up.

Scarlet laughed. "Is that what scared you? A black cat?"

"N-no," I stammered.

The cat tilted its head to one side and stared up at me without blinking.

It's not a cat, Scarlet, I thought, my heart pounding. *It's some kind of shadow creature from the house. I didn't imagine it. This is not really a cat.*

Scarlet tugged my T-shirt sleeve. "Let's go. Don't you know you can't win a staring contest with a cat?"

Before I could move, the cat hissed at me and swiped a paw in the air.

I jumped back.

My sister laughed. "That cat doesn't like you."

"I don't like it, either," I whispered. I squinted down at it and tried to read its eyes. I knew I was right about it.

"Get over it," Scarlet said. "You can't be afraid of a black cat, Riley. Look how tame and sweet it is."

I watched it spin away from me, raising its tail high behind it. The cat loped off through the tall weeds, then silently padded over the grass toward the mansion.

And as it ran, it appeared to dissolve. It just melted away. Poof. It became a blob of smoke again. When it neared the mansion, floating over the lawn, it faded into a flickering shadow.

Then I gasped as the shadow exploded. It burst apart, into a million pieces. Like dandelion seeds when you blow on them. I stood frozen, watching the tiny bits of shadow blow apart, float high over the grass, and disappear.

"Did you see that, Scarlet?" I screamed. "Did you see that?"

She was bent over, picking my backpack up from where I'd dropped it. "See *what*, Riley?"

"The cat—it—it—" I sputtered.

"It ran away. So what?"

"No. You don't understand. The cat—" I stopped with my mouth hanging open. I squinted into the shadowy light to the low stone wall that ran along the back of the yard.

Something moved along the wall.

There was someone there. A girl. Standing very still, under a tree that overhung the wall.

I squinted harder. "Who is *that*?"

"Let's find out," Scarlet said. She jumped over a fallen tree branch and began walking toward the girl.

I hesitated.

Scarlet turned back. "You're not *scared* of her, too, are you? Are you going to throw yourself on the ground and start hyperventilating again?"

I could feel my face turning red. "Okay, okay. Give me a break."

I knew what I'd seen was real. But what was the point of arguing with Scarlet? She was twelve minutes older than me. That meant she had to win every argument and be right all the time.

The girl watched us as we made our way to her. Her blond hair sparkled in a splash of sunlight. Even from a distance, I could see she was very pale. She looked about our age, short and very thin.

She wore a white top and blue skirt that came

down to her knees. She had both hands tucked into the pockets of her skirt.

"Hey," Scarlet called. "Hi."

The girl removed one hand from a pocket and gave us a short wave. She was very pretty, I thought. Dark eyes. Her smile slowly spread over her face.

Why is she standing against the back wall of Shudder Mansion?

As we stepped close, her smile grew wider. Her blond hair fluttered in a gust of wind.

"Hi," Scarlet said. "How's it going? I'm Scarlet and he's Riley."

"My name is Mia," she said. She had a soft, whispery voice. It seemed to come from deep in her throat.

"We were just taking a shortcut through the back lawn here," I said.

"We live two blocks over there," Scarlet explained, pointing in the direction of our house. "Are you new here?"

Mia nodded. "My family just moved in. Two blocks that way," she said in her throaty whisper and pointed in the opposite direction.

"What are you doing back here?" I blurted out.

Scarlet gave me a look. Like, *What kind of question is that? Mia has every right to be here, too.*

Mia shrugged. "Just exploring. I don't know the neighborhood at all."

15

Scarlet started to say something, but I interrupted. "Did you see that black cat?"

Mia shook her head. "No. I didn't see a cat."

Scarlet frowned at me. "Riley, give us a break. It was just a black cat. No one is interested."

Mia studied me. "Are you afraid of black cats?"

I shrugged. "Not really," I answered. "You just wandered back here? Did anyone tell you about this house?"

Scarlet rolled her eyes.

I didn't care. Mia was new in the neighborhood. She should be warned. "Do you believe in evil spirits?" I said. "Do you believe a whole house can be evil?"

Mia laughed. She had a high, tinkly laugh. Kind of musical. "I don't think so."

"Well, this place is called—"

"Don't listen to my brother," Scarlet interrupted. "He's obsessed with the video game about this old house. It's called *Escape from Shudder Mansion*. Have you heard of it?"

Mia tugged a strand of blond hair. "I don't think so. I'm not too into video games."

"Well, Riley plays it for hours," Scarlet said. "It's all about this old mansion and how evil it is. Riley is obsessed with the game—and he's started to believe it."

"A *lot* of people believe it!" I snapped. "I'm not crazy." I was tired of Scarlet making fun of me. And I didn't think she should start telling Mia how stupid I was for believing the stories about the mansion.

Okay. Maybe I had an instant crush on Mia. Maybe I didn't want my sister to embarrass me in front of her. Maybe. That's all I'm saying.

I realized Mia was still studying me. "So what do you believe is inside the mansion?" she asked.

"Evil spirits," I said. "They once were human. But they were turned into shadow creatures. They can be human. Or they can be monsters. They're trapped inside the mansion. There's no way they can get out. And they wait for someone to come inside. So they can take their revenge on the world that trapped them."

Mia laughed. "Sounds like a horror movie or something."

"I warned you," Scarlet said.

Mia raised her eyes to the mansion. "Is there really a video game about this old abandoned mansion?"

I nodded. "It might be the scariest game ever made. And it all takes place right in our neighborhood."

Mia's eyes burned into mine. "Would you be afraid to go into the mansion? Would you ever, like, dare to go inside?"

Her question caught me by surprise. The answer was *no*. But I didn't want Mia to think I was a wimp.

17

"Yeah. I'd go inside," I said. "But I'd probably like for some of my friends to come with me."

Scarlet rolled her eyes, then turned away to wave to some kids she knew.

Mia laughed.

And as Mia laughed, something weird happened. She changed.

Her pale skin seemed to fade away. I mean, I could see right through it. I could see right through her skin—into her skull!

As she laughed, I could see her bony skull. I stared in horror at her skeletal grin. Her eyes disappeared. Her eyeballs sank back into their sockets until the sockets appeared like two deep holes in the front of her skull.

Her teeth now looked crooked and cracked.

And her lips . . . Her lips were *gone*!

She stood there, hands in pockets, a skull. A laughing, eyeless skull.

I couldn't hold it in. I couldn't stop the scream that burst from deep inside me.

"NOOOOOOOOOOO!"

5

Scarlet turned and dove for me. She grabbed me again. She squeezed my shoulders and shook me hard. It was getting to be a habit.

"Riley, what is your *problem*?" she demanded.

I turned and stared over my sister's shoulder at Mia. Mia with her blond hair, and pretty dark eyes, and nice smile. Mia nice and normal again.

Am I cracking up? Totally losing it?

No, I'm not.

I know I'm not crazy.

But . . .

I had to cover up somehow. I'd just let out a deafening scream of horror. "Uh . . . something bit me," I said. I scratched my ankle. "Hope it wasn't a spider."

Lame. I know. But it was the best I could do.

I gazed at Mia, waiting for her to change again. I knew I had seen right through her skin. I couldn't get the picture of her empty eye sockets and cracked, missing teeth out of my mind. I saw her laughing her skeletal, open-jawed laugh.

I saw right through her face.

Suddenly, I was even more desperate to get away from Shudder Mansion. Scarlet and Mia were talking, but I didn't hear a word. I wanted to get far away from the creepy old place and Mia as fast as I could.

I wanted to talk to Scarlet. To ask her if she saw anything strange about this girl. Something was definitely weird about her. I had to talk to my sister about it.

Standing so close to Shudder Mansion was totally freaking me out. I had the sudden feeling that I might explode in another scream. Okay. I know I needed to calm down. I panic easily. It's a problem. I'm working on it.

I grabbed Scarlet's hand and started to tug her away. I couldn't believe it when I heard her invite Mia over to our house for dinner.

No. Please don't bring her to our house, I pleaded silently.

There's something very wrong here. Something horrible is going to happen.

"Come home with us now," Scarlet was saying. "I think we're having spaghetti. Do you like spaghetti?"

Mia nodded. She glanced over Scarlet's shoulder at me.

I forced a smile to my face. "Awesome," I murmured.

"Okay. Thank you," Mia said.

And the next thing I knew, the three of us were walking along the sidewalk to my house, talking as if everything were just peachy, perfectly fine.

Until we crossed the street and our house came into view. And Mia suddenly turned to me and demanded, "Riley? Why do you keep looking at me like that?"

The question caught me completely by surprise. I let out a burst of nervous laughter.

"Me? Haha. I wasn't looking at you. The... uh... sun was in my eyes."

Lame, again. I'm not the best liar in the world.

She kept her eyes narrowed at me. I couldn't tell what she was thinking.

Scarlet gave her a tug. "Come on. Don't pay attention to him. He got freaked out by a black cat, and he's been weird ever since."

"I'm not afraid of black cats," I muttered.

I followed them into the house. I couldn't wait to take my sister aside. Mia sat down in the den. I pulled Scarlet into the kitchen.

"Riley, what is it?" she asked in a loud whisper.

I tugged her away from the kitchen doorway. "There's something very wrong about Mia," I whispered. "Did you see—?"

Scarlet put a finger over my lips. "I'm sorry you're having a bad day, Riley. But you've got to stop this crazy talk."

I pushed her finger away. "It isn't crazy," I insisted. "You didn't see anything strange? Like when the sun shone behind her and you could see her skull?"

Scarlet's mouth dropped open, but she didn't say anything. Finally, she said, "I'm not even going to answer that."

I glanced at the door to make sure Mia wasn't standing there. "Why did you invite her over here?"

"Because she just moved here, and she doesn't know anyone," Scarlet answered. "Did you see how lonely she looked, standing there by herself in the backyard of the mansion?"

"Why was she standing there?" I demanded. "Why—"

Scarlet pushed her finger against my lips again. "I'm going to be her friend and show her around," she said. "So stop staring at her and making her feel uncomfortable."

"I—I—I—" I sputtered.

Scarlet lowered her hand to my shoulder. "You need to chill out, Riley. You're totally stressed. It was that black cat, wasn't it. You're cataphobic, aren't you."

"Huh? Cataphobic?"

"I think that's a word," she said. She pointed to the stairs. "Go upstairs and play your video game. It's the only thing that relaxes you."

"But, Mia—"

"Leave us girls alone." She gave me a push toward the stairs. "Go into your fantasy world and let Mia and me get to know one another."

I shrugged and started toward the stairs. I knew I wasn't going to get anywhere with Scarlet. And I was happy to get away from Mia for at least a little while.

My room was kind of a mess. That morning, I tried to make a neat pile of my dirty clothes on the floor next to the closet. But somehow dirty clothes never want to go into a neat pile. They want to spread all over the floor.

I had a nightmare the night before and tossed all my covers off the bed. They were still bunched up on the floor. I probably should have picked them up. But I was eager to get back to the game.

I know. I know. I had a few terrifying moments this afternoon at the *real* Shudder Mansion. So why was I so desperate to get back to that frightening house in the video game?

Scarlet was right. It's just about the only thing that relaxes me. I'm a tight guitar string, remember. But for some reason, exploring the dark, twisting halls of Shudder Mansion, and battling all of the shadowy monsters and villains that come racing at me . . . well . . . it makes me feel good. I guess it makes me forget what's troubling me. And I can always stop when I want to.

Does that make any sense?

I started the game up. I was on level four. I found myself standing at the top of one of the tall towers. I mean, my avatar was standing there. On the screen, I was a tall blond knight in a royal blue cloak and matching tights.

I hadn't earned my armor yet. I was still two levels away from winning the proper protection for a knight.

It was silent in the tower. A flickering torch on the wall gave out the only light. The shadows seemed to dance all around me.

Silence. I turned up the volume a little on the game controller. I could hear fluttering sounds from outside the tower. Bats?

I gripped the controller tightly. My hand was already sweaty even though I had just started to play. I knew I wouldn't be alone in the tower for long.

Yes. I heard a stab of low music. A warning. I moved the controller so I could see all around me. I could turn 360 degrees, spin all around the room, and see everything in it.

I stopped at the steep stone stairs. Yes. Yes.

A shadow crept slowly and silently up the stairs. I sucked in a deep breath. I knew it was coming for me. It was coming for a fight. The shadow wouldn't stay a shadow. It would stand up or spread out or float off the floor and become a terrifying creature, one of the creatures trapped forever in Shudder Mansion.

I fought back my fear. What weapon should I choose? I had only seconds to decide. The shadow was already changing, growing tall, making sick gurgling sounds as it transformed.

I didn't have many weapons to choose from. I'd lost all my swords and knives in a battle with a deadly cobra. I had a thick rope, and an armored shield, and a pole with a deadly laser ray that could only be used once.

I grabbed the shield. Maybe I could use it to shove the creature away. Maybe I could use it to flatten it against the wall.

This definitely wasn't the right weapon to defeat it.

If only I hadn't lost my swords and knives.

I squeezed the controller as the shadowy figure reached the top step. It started to change. The deep shadow parted. A monster started to climb out.

I could see round black eyes, shiny in the torchlight. A long snout. Jagged rows of teeth. An alligator head, snapping—snapping its long jaw. It rose up on two legs—like a human—an alligator head on a human body.

I watched it grow taller . . . taller . . . till it was taller than me.

"YEEEEEEEEEEE!"

It opened its alligator jaws wide and uttered a deafening screech as it dove toward me.

I ducked. Its heavy head thumped my shoulder. I nearly fell to my knees.

I swung the shield around and tried to stab it at the creature's wide middle. But the creature floated out of my reach—and came at me again with another terrifying screech.

I dipped the controller and made my avatar roll across the floor. I pulled up the shield as the creature moved to climb onto me. I gave it a hard shove—and sent it spinning back to the wall.

As I struggled to climb to my feet, it let out an ugly hiss and prepared to dive at me again. Its eyes reflected the flickering light as it snapped its big jaws. Once. Twice. Then it lifted one of its massive legs and swiped the shield right from my hand.

I lunged for the shield—but stopped.

This shield isn't going to help me. The creature is going to eat me alive.

I frantically pressed a button on the controller and traded weapons. I wrapped my hand around the laser pole. This was a dangerous move. I knew I had only enough power to use it once.

My timing had to be perfect. I had to send the laser ray into the creature's heart. Or I would be alligator food in less than a minute.

27

It roared again, raised itself high, and came at me.

I fired the laser. Missed. The beam hit the tower ceiling and bounced off. The pole made a fizzling sound, like air going out of a balloon.

The creature snapped its jaws, ready for its meal.

In a last desperate move, I pulled back my arm—and heaved the pole at it.

The creature made a wheezing sound as the pole slid into its open mouth—and stuck there. The startled monster stood there for a few seconds with the handle of the pole jutting out from its mouth.

Then, as I stared in amazement, it made ugly choking sounds. Its eyes rolled up. It disappeared into shadow again. Grew smaller . . . smaller . . . until it was like a puddle of ink. A puddle that oozed back down the stairs.

Victory!

I pumped both fists in the air and let out a happy cheer.

Now the game would offer me a new reward. What would it be? A new weapon? A new superpower?

I turned back to the screen. My avatar was now standing in a bright room with long gold drapes, a huge crystal chandelier, and a plush red carpet.

I moved the controller so I could see all around the room—and stopped at a big gold cup standing on a narrow table. The gold cup looked like a trophy. It shimmered and glowed under the bright light from the chandelier.

This was my reward for defeating the alligator creature. I was a little disappointed. I wanted a new weapon. But I knew the cup would probably come in handy later in the game.

I moved my avatar closer to accept the cup.

And stopped when I saw something dark poking around the lip of the cup. Was the cup filled with something?

As I moved forward again—enormous, ugly black spiders came pouring out. *Hundreds* of spiders . . . so unnaturally huge . . . spiders nearly the size of *mice*. They stampeded from the cup, clambering on top of each other, their legs a spindly, churning tangle.

To my shock, they *leaped* from the gold cup—as if they could fly!

I didn't stand a chance. Before I could step back, they were on me . . . climbing over my shoulders . . . my chest . . . their stick-thin legs poking my cheeks, my forehead, covering my face.

I'm doomed. The gold cup wasn't a prize—it was a TRAP.

Game over.

I dropped to my knees on the carpet. The fat

spiders swarmed over me. I moved the controller, trying to swipe them away with both arms.

And then . . . another figure entered the scene. A woman. No. A girl.

She waved a silver wand in the air. Waved it once . . . twice . . . And the spiders slid off me. I stared at the screen as they scampered away, their legs poking the carpet, fat bodies bobbing as they ran.

I raised my avatar to his feet. And turned him toward the girl who had rescued him.

And let out a startled cry.

I nearly dropped the controller. I squinted at the girl on the screen.

Mia?

Is that really Mia in the game?

I paused the game with the girl in the middle of the screen. I jumped off the bed and walked closer. My heart began to pound. I stared hard.

Yes. It was Mia. She was there, in the *Shudder Mansion* game.

But—how? How could that be?

I bolted for the bedroom door. I tripped over the pile of dirty clothes. Caught my balance. Ran out into the hall. And shouted down the stairs:

"Scarlet? Scarlet! Come upstairs! *Hurry!*"

7

I knew there was something weird about Mia. But Scarlet didn't want to believe me.

Now she HAD to.

I waited in the hall, my heart pounding. I heard the thud of footsteps. Then Scarlet and Mia appeared, running up the stairs.

I know your secret, Mia, I thought. *I knew there was something weird about you. And now I've got proof!*

"Riley? What's wrong?" Scarlet called.

"I—I'll show you," I stammered. I motioned them into my room.

Scarlet narrowed her eyes at me. "What did you want to show us? That mountain of dirty clothes on the floor? Very impressive."

Mia was gazing at the *Star Trek* posters on my wall. "These are nice," she said.

"Never mind the posters," I said. I pointed to the figure frozen on the screen. "Look. Look carefully."

"At the game?" Scarlet asked.

"At the face on the screen." I walked up close and pointed. "Look. Look who it is."

Scarlet stepped up beside me and squinted at it. She didn't say anything.

Mia turned away from the posters and walked over.

Here's my proof, Mia, I thought. *How are you going to explain this?*

When she saw the girl on the screen, Mia's eyes went wide. Then she burst out laughing.

"Oh, wow!" she exclaimed. "That girl looks a little like me. She really does look like me."

Scarlet finally caught on. "Yes. She does. She looks like you. The same blond hair and round, dark eyes."

Mia shook her head, her eyes on the screen. "Is that what you wanted to show us, Riley? That's a riot." She bumped knuckles with Scarlet. "Hey, I'm a *star*! I'm a video game star!"

They both laughed. But I didn't think it was funny.

"But—but—" I sputtered. "It's really you!"

For some reason, that made them laugh harder.

"I'm not that pretty," Mia said. She smiled at me. "I think it's so cute that she reminds you of me, Riley."

Cute?

Why wouldn't they take me seriously?

"Mom says it's almost dinnertime," Scarlet said. "If you see *me* in your game, too, call me."

Ha Ha. Big joker.

She and Mia headed back downstairs.

I stared at the girl on the screen. I knew I wasn't crazy. It looked exactly like Mia. She even had the same smile.

I started the game up again. Did the girl on the screen have the same soft, whispery voice as Mia? If she did, that would convince me even more that it *was* Mia.

But the girl didn't speak. After she waved the spiders away, she vanished from the room. I was left standing there with the gold cup shining on its table.

Was I supposed to take the gold cup now that it was empty?

I couldn't decide. It was hard to concentrate on the game. I couldn't stop thinking about Mia.

Finally, I moved my avatar forward and made him grab the gold cup. Then I spun him around to the doorway.

A few steps toward the doorway—and then I stopped. Another shadow rolled into view. It floated close to the floor, curling on itself, shaped like a long snake.

What weapon should I use?

Will this gold cup help me?

I had no time to think about it. The shadow

moved quickly, swirling over itself, coiling and uncoiling, silent as a slithering snake.

And then it changed shape completely. And I stared at the screen—stared at a black cat at my feet.

A black cat with green eyes.

A black cat that formed from a shadow. The same thing I'd seen just an hour ago outside Shudder Mansion.

No. Impossible.

First Mia. Then the black cat.

No. It couldn't be.

Could it?

I didn't know it then. But I was soon going to find out the answer to that question—on the most terrifying night of my life.

SLAPPY HERE, EVERYONE.

I'm like Riley. I like to play games, too. Would you like to play a game with me? How about an old-fashioned game of *Hide and Shriek*! Hahaha.

My favorite game is called *Scare the Reader to Death*! Want to know how to play it? Just keep reading!

We all know that Riley is going to end up inside Shudder Mansion, don't we? But once he's there, will it be GAME OVER for him? Hahaha.

Let's change the scene and go to his classroom the next day. I have a feeling things are going to get *strange* . . .

I sat at my desk in the back row and listened to Carter Burwasser. He stood at the front of the class, reading his report about his family's vacation on safari in Africa.

Carter had a toothy grin pasted on his face. And in the sunlight from the open window, his big round head glowed like a pumpkin.

Actually, Carter is blond and very pink. Like a pink balloon with a nose and eyes.

Maybe you can tell that I don't like Carter Burwasser very much.

Well, I've got good reasons. Carter thinks he's hot stuff.

He is a bragger and a snob, and he thinks he's better than anyone else. Sure, he gets all A's, and the teachers love him. But what does *that* mean?

You should see the way he struts around the halls, like he's on parade or something. Like he's a star and everyone is staring at him.

He thinks he's awesome looking, tossing his wavy blond hair from side to side, winking at all the girls with his bright blue eyes. I'm not joking. He flirts with every girl in the sixth grade.

Everything about him makes my teeth itch. Am I jealous of him? Of course not. Why would I be jealous of a pink balloon face?

There are so many things to hate about him.

I guess the worst was the day he brought his pet llama to school. He brought it onto the playground and let everyone pet it and feed it.

The llama stepped on Mrs. Blume's foot. She's our teacher, and I know it really hurt. But she just put a tight smile on her face and said she was fine.

Just because it was Carter and everything he does is wonderful.

And why does he have a pet llama in the first place? Just to show off.

I can't have a dog or a cat because my parents are allergic. And there he is, taking his llama for walks around the neighborhood every day.

But I'm not jealous. Don't think I'm jealous. I don't even *want* a stupid llama.

I was sitting there in class, thinking about the llama and only half-listening to Carter's safari story. But then the story got interesting—because Carter was in major danger. So I started to listen harder.

"It was a very dark night," Carter read from his paper. "And our tent was sweating from the heat and humidity."

Nice detail, Carter. I could tell by the smile on Mrs. Blume's face that she really appreciated that.

"I lay there on my cot listening to the strange calls of night birds in the trees," he continued. "Then I heard footsteps. It sounded like someone was trying to get into our tent."

Our classroom was silent now. Mrs. Blume sat forward at her desk, hands clasped on the desktop, listening intently.

"I went outside to investigate," Carter read, holding the pages of his report close to his pink face. "At first, I didn't see anything. So I took a few steps away from our tent. That was my big mistake."

He turned the page slowly, trying to create suspense, I guess.

I glanced across the room at my sister, Scarlet. She agrees with me that Carter is a creep. But she was wide-eyed as she listened to his story.

"The next thing I knew, there was a big creature behind me," Carter read. "It was huge and black and its eyes glowed in the moonlight. It took me a few seconds to recognize it—a black rhino."

A few kids gasped. Carter continued: "It bumped my back with its curved horn. I tried to scream but no sound came out of my mouth. The big rhino raised its head to bump me again. So I took off running."

"Wow. Scary," Mrs. Blume murmured.

"I was so scared, my legs felt like Jell-O," Carter read. "But I ran as fast as I could. I ran around our whole circle of tents, and the black rhino followed. There were patches of moonlight on the ground. All the rest was total blackness."

Carter grinned at Mrs. Blume. "Here's where it gets totally scary," he told her. He began reading again. "The camp was surrounded by wilderness. I didn't want to leave the circle of tents. But the rhino was closing in on me. I knew I couldn't run much farther."

He glanced at the teacher to make sure she was enjoying it. "And then I tripped over a tent pole. I tripped and went down with a thud. Fell onto my stomach. I tried to roll over. To climb back up. But I was too frightened to move."

"What did the rhino do?" Mrs. Blume demanded.

"The rhino watched me on the ground," Carter said. "Then it made a grunting sound. Really gross. It turned around and walked away. I guess it got interested in something else."

What a disappointing ending. Too bad the rhino didn't eat Carter whole. Then I wouldn't have to be here, listening to him.

"Or maybe I scared it away," Carter said. "I *did* wave my arms at it and shout for it to go away. And gave it a really mean look. I think I was brave after all. I think maybe I *stared* it away."

Sure you did.

"That's a wonderful piece of writing," Mrs. Blume said. She motioned for the class to give Carter some applause, and everyone obediently clapped.

Carter turned even more pink. His grin was so wide, it looked like he had four rows of teeth.

"You must have worked really hard on that essay," the teacher said.

Carter shook his head. "Oh no. Not really. I just knocked it out in a few minutes. I'm a fast writer."

Carter strutted back to his seat. Mrs. Blume climbed to her feet and stepped away from the desk. "I know all of you kids would like to have a big adventure like Carter, *wouldn't* you?" she asked.

No one answered. I think we were all waiting to hear what she had in mind.

"That's your next assignment," she said. "Your next assignment is to have an adventure."

Some hands shot up. "What do you mean, 'have an adventure'?" Scarlet's friend Danitia asked.

"I'm going to divide you into groups," Mrs. Blume replied. "And I want you to make documentary videos about an adventure, about something exciting that you're going to do."

"You mean we go out looking for an adventure?" Scarlet asked. "Like we try to find a black rhino to chase us down Maple Street?"

Everyone laughed.

"We'll plan the adventure in advance," the teacher answered. "We'll prepare for it. Get you ready. Then you can record the exciting things that happen to you."

Carter raised his hand. "Do I have to do it—since I already had an adventure?"

"Yes, everyone has to do it," Mrs. Blume said.

The class started to buzz, everyone talking at once. Some kids had ideas for adventures. I couldn't think of anything. I mean, Middleview Village is a pretty boring town.

"How about spending a night in the mummy room at the museum?" someone asked.

"I like that," Mrs. Blume said.

"Could we stay up all night in the zoo?" Danitia asked.

"That might work," the teacher answered.

I suddenly realized she had her eyes on me. Why was she watching me? Was she waiting for me to come up with a scary adventure? I didn't have a clue.

She stared for a while longer. I could see she was thinking hard. "Riley, I have the perfect idea for you," she said finally.

I felt a sudden chill. I didn't like the smile on her face.

"You're always talking about that video game you play," she said. "And you write papers about it. And you paint pictures of the old mansion in art class. You're obsessed with it—right?"

"I . . . guess," I said softly.

"Well, I have the perfect adventure for you. Why don't you spend a night in Shudder Mansion?"

"That sounds awesome. But do I have to do it all by myself?" I said. My voice cracked. Some kids laughed.

A wave of panic rolled down my body. Was she serious?

"No. Not by yourself," Mrs. Blume said. "I told you, I'm going to divide the class into groups. I'll pick five others to stay in Shudder Mansion with you. How's that?"

"I . . . uh . . . well . . ." I was terrified by the whole idea. I knew there were evil spirits in the house. All kinds of horrifying creatures, like that black shadow cat that had floated out of the mansion yesterday. And the half-man, half-alligator I had to fight in the game. What if he was real, too?

I began to imagine all the horrible things that could happen to kids who tried to stay in that house all night. I didn't have to imagine—I knew them all from the video game!

I wanted to say, *"No way. NO WAY I'll go in that old house at night. That's not an adventure. That's suicide!"*

But I suddenly realized that everyone in class was looking at me. Watching to see if I'd be brave or if I'd be a total chicken-wimp.

"That sounds awesome!" I said. "That'll be the best adventure of all. I can't wait. Can we do it tonight?"

Please change your mind. Please change your mind.

Mrs. Blume chuckled. "Maybe next week, Riley. We have to get organized." She sat down on the edge of her desk. "Let's choose your team first."

She glanced around the room. "Are there any volunteers?"

No hands went up.

"Scarlet, would you like to join your brother?"

My sister thought about it for a long moment. "Okay. I'll go. But it's just a dark, empty mansion. I don't think there will be anything exciting."

Boy is she wrong, I thought. *If she had believed me about the shadow that snaked along the grass and became a black cat. If she had listened to me about Mia . . . she'd know how wrong she is.*

"How about you, Theresa?" Mrs. Blume asked. Theresa was a quiet, shy girl who always liked

44

to sit in the back row in a corner. She almost never talked.

"I'm not allowed to stay out late," she said softly. I could barely hear her. "My mom is a librarian at the Middleview Village library. I'll bet she'd let a bunch of us stay all night in the stacks at the library. It's supposed to be haunted."

"That might be fun," Mrs. Blume said. "Let's keep that in mind for you, Theresa."

Mrs. Blume shielded her eyes with a hand to her forehead and looked around the room again. "How about you, Cheng? Want to join the Shudder Mansion team?"

Cheng Lee was another quiet, shy kid. He was the smallest kid in our class. He really looked like a fourth grader, like someone's younger brother. He had a funny laugh, sort of a chipmunk laugh, and everyone liked him because, even though he didn't say much, he was always really cheerful and a good guy.

"Okay," he said. "I'll do it. But . . . can I bring a flashlight?"

"I think you'll want to bring all kinds of equipment," Mrs. Blume told him.

She turned to my sister's friend, Danitia. "You and Scarlet hang out all the time. Do you want to hang out with her in Shudder Mansion?"

A grin spread over Danitia's face. "Not really. But I guess I'll do it."

"That's a good friend," Mrs. Blume said. "And very brave."

"I hope I don't have to be *too* brave," Danitia said, and everyone laughed.

"Okay. We need one more victim. I mean, team member," Mrs. Blume said. She gazed around the room, studying each face.

Please don't pick Carter, I thought. *Please, Mrs. Blume—don't pick Carter.*

The moment I had that thought, Carter began waving his hand wildly in the air. "I'll do it! I'll go!" he shouted. "I've already shown how brave I am. They need someone like me."

Please . . . please . . .

"Okay, Carter," Mrs. Blume said. "You're on the team."

Carter pumped both fists in the air in triumph.

I sank down in my seat with a groan. Stuck all night in Shudder Mansion with that show-off, Carter Burwasser. Not fair.

Mrs. Blume stood up and stretched her back.

Cheng had his hand raised. She nodded at him.

"We all know the stories about Shudder Mansion," he said. "About how some evil people died in there and their spirits are still inside. How they can transform into monsters, and stuff like that."

Cheng hesitated. He had a frightened look on

his face. His hands gripped the desktop. "Do you think those stories are true?"

"Maybe," Mrs. Blume answered.

"So . . ." Cheng hesitated again. "So, if we spend a night in there, Mrs. Blume, will we . . . will we be safe?"

"Yes. *Will* we?" Danitia added.

"No, you won't," Mrs. Blume answered. "That's the assignment. You're all going to be in horrible danger. Some of you probably won't survive."

10

Those words sent a hush over the room.

Mrs. Blume laughed. "I'm joking," she said. "Did you really think I was serious?" She shook her head. "This is a school, remember. It's not our job to send you off into real danger." She laughed again.

She doesn't know the truth about Shudder Mansion, I told myself. *She's like Scarlet. She thinks the stories are fake.*

"Of course we'll make sure you are safe," she said. "In fact, your parents can go along with you. They can have the same exciting adventures that you do."

Uh-oh. My parents wouldn't want to go. They're allergic to dust, for one thing. Mom would hate being in a dirty old house. She's a clean freak. Everything in our house sparkles as if it were just dipped in polish.

And Dad has a thing about insects. He got a bunch of bad spider bites on his face when he was little, and he's been freaked out by insects ever since. We can't ever go on a picnic because Dad doesn't even feel comfortable around *ants*!

So I'd be amazed if my parents said yes.

I was thinking about them and didn't even realize that Carter was talking. I tuned back in. He seemed to be talking about special equipment for our adventure.

"My parents bought me this paranormal detection kit," he was saying. "I'm probably the only one in town who has it. It's professional, see. I'll bring it to Shudder Mansion, and maybe we can get some audio or video of actual spirits in the house."

He's going to ruin everything, I thought. *He'll spend the whole night bragging about his detection kit and making us all pay attention to it. And he'll be the star of the night.*

"It's just like the one they use on TV," Carter continued. "It's very complicated and delicate, but I know how to use it."

"That's wonderful, Carter," Mrs. Blume said. "You know I always appreciate your enthusiasm."

"I always like to give 110 percent," Carter replied.

Don't you just want to punch him?

After school, Scarlet had a guitar lesson, so I wandered off by myself. It was a warm day for fall. The sun beamed down from a cloudless sky.

49

Everything—the grass, the trees, the houses along the street, the cars and SUVs rolling by—seemed too bright to be real.

I crossed the street and found myself gazing up at Shudder Mansion. I hadn't meant to walk here. I stopped and, for a moment, had the feeling that something ... some power ... had pulled me here. Pulled me here against my will.

And just as I thought that, a hand grabbed me, and hard fingers wrapped around the back of my neck. And a raspy voice whispered in my ear: *"You will DIE in Shudder Mansion!"*

I opened my mouth and let out a high, shrill scream of fright.

I jerked free of the hard grip, twisted away, and spun around. And stared at a grinning Carter Burwasser. "Did I scare you?" he asked.

"I knew it was you," I lied.

His grin grew wider. "Then why did you scream?"

"I didn't scream," I said. "I just pretended to scream." Lame. I know. But I couldn't admit the truth—that he'd scared me to death.

My heart was still pounding. I could still hear those whispered words in my ear.

Why did everyone think Shudder Mansion was a big joke?

I guessed it was because I'm the only one who plays the *Shudder Mansion* video game. I'm the only one who knows the kind of horrors that might be waiting inside the old house.

Carter and I stared up at the back of the mansion. The whole world all around us was bright and green and sunny. But the mansion rose like a dark creature. The walls were dark as charcoal and the rows of windows even blacker.

I felt a chill. The air seemed at least ten degrees colder up close to the mansion.

"Are you pumped about spending the night here?" Carter asked.

"No way," I replied. "The stories about this place—"

He laughed. "You don't believe them—*do* you?"

I hesitated. "Carter, do you ever play the video game?"

A sneer crossed his pink face. "No, I don't play games. I write my own. Don't you know programming code? I've been coding since I was nine."

"I play the *Shudder Mansion* game a lot," I said. "And it's very disturbing. If any of it is true . . ."

"I have night vision goggles I'm going to bring," Carter interrupted. "It's the kind the army uses in combat. Riley, do you have your own pair? If you don't, I can bring you a pair."

"No, I don't have that," I murmured.

Is there anything Carter DOESN'T have?

"The goggles are awesome," Carter said. "It makes everything seem bright as day. You can see a mouse blink its eye."

"I don't *want* to see a mouse blink its eye," I said.

Carter laughed. For some reason, he thought everything I said was a joke. He laughed at almost everything I said.

I *told* you he was annoying.

I just wanted to lose him and hurry home. But I heard voices. I turned around—and there came Scarlet, Danitia, and Cheng across the back lawn. Our whole team.

"We knew you'd be here, Riley," Scarlet called.

"What happened to your guitar lesson?" I asked.

"Canceled. Derek has the flu."

"I was just telling him some of the excellent equipment I'm going to bring when we stay all night," Carter said. "I have a glow-in-the-dark backpack so I can always find it."

"Cool," Cheng said. "I'm bringing glow-in-the-dark water bottles. I get really thirsty."

I thought Cheng was joking, but I couldn't tell.

Danitia motioned to the back door. "Why don't we go inside right now? You know. Check the place out in the daytime."

"No way," I said. I guess I said it too quickly. I must have sounded a little scared. They were all staring at me. "Uh . . . we don't want to spoil the adventure," I added. Pretty fast thinking.

"What kind of adventure will it be if our parents are there?" Danitia asked, rolling her eyes. "We have to find a way to lose them. Seriously."

"I'm kind of glad the parents are coming," Cheng said. "You know. In case there is some kind of emergency."

Carter laughed. "Like an evil spirit grabbing us and pulling us into a world of darkness."

I felt a chill at the back of my neck. I didn't like Carter making jokes about this. I could see he wasn't going to take it seriously.

"Let's take a walk all around the mansion. We need to find the best escape route," I said, thinking about the shadow that had turned into the black cat.

Carter laughed again. I wanted to push my hand over his grinning mouth. "Riley is already planning to run away," he said.

Scarlet and Danitia thought that was funny. Cheng slapped me on the back. "You lead the way, boss," he said. He calls everyone *boss*. I don't really know what he means by it.

I started to walk along the back wall of the house. The dark shingles were cracked and broken. I tripped over a small rock hidden by the tall weeds that filled the yard.

We passed some low windows at the side of the house. They were so caked with dust, I couldn't see inside.

What is in there? I wondered. *What is in there waiting for us?*

I stopped to gaze up at the attic windows high above, and the others got ahead of me.

"Hey, wait up," I called.

Danitia and Scarlet were yakking away, the way they always do, and didn't hear me.

Moving away from the dark wall, I began to walk toward the front of the giant mansion. I stepped into a bright pool of sunlight. I raised a hand to shield my eyes from the glare.

I stopped and glanced down at my long shadow spreading across the weeds.

Whoa. Wait.

I'd stopped walking—but my shadow hadn't!

My mouth dropped open and I gasped for air. I watched my shadow stretch across the weeds. It grew longer . . . longer . . . even though I was frozen in place.

My shadow was moving without me!

"Hey—" I tried to call to the others. But they had turned the corner. "Hey!" My voice came out in a choked whisper.

The sun beamed down hot on the top of my head. I shielded my eyes with both hands—and watched my shadow stretch and roll in front of me. And as I stared at it, it changed shape.

It formed a fat, ugly lizard. A lizard with an enormous head. I saw the shadow of a flickering tongue. The monstrous head darted from side to side.

It wasn't my shadow anymore!

"Hey, everyone—*stop*!" I finally found my voice. "Stop!" I screamed. "Hey—look! My shadow! Hurry! Come back! My shadow!"

12

As I motioned frantically, they came running around the side of the house. "Riley—what's wrong?" Scarlet called.

"My . . . my shadow!" I stammered, pointing at the ground.

Scarlet and Danitia were wide-eyed as they ran. Carter and Cheng trotted behind them. The sky darkened suddenly. The sun faded behind a broad, gray cloud—and my shadow disappeared with it.

"What's the problem?" Cheng asked. "Are you okay?"

"I—I—" I sputtered. "My shadow—it moved. It was a lizard monster!"

Carter grinned. "Hey. I can do shadow animals, too. Do you know how to make a duck?" He put his hands together and went, "Quack quack."

The cloud passed and the sunlight washed over us again. Carter's shadow duck slid over the weeds. My shadow was back to normal. I

57

stared hard at it, waiting for it to move . . . to stretch again. But no. It was just my shadow, rippling a little as the weeds shifted in the breeze.

"Riley, what's up with you?" Danitia asked. "If you want to scare us, you'll have to come up with something better than *that*."

"I . . . I'm not trying to scare you," I stammered. "My shadow moved without me, and—and—"

Scarlet was squinting hard at me. "Riley, how come all the rest of us didn't have a shadow problem? Why does something weird happen to you every time we walk near the mansion? But nothing happens to me or to anyone else? Why are you the only one who sees these things?"

"Maybe because he's crazy?" Carter suggested. He put his hands together to make another duck shadow and shoved his hands right up to my face. "Quaaaack quaaaack." His fingers pinched my nose.

Everyone thought that was a riot.

I didn't have an answer to my sister's questions. Why was I the only one to see these things? Maybe because I was the only one who played the *Shudder Mansion* game? Maybe that had something to do with it.

"Let's see if we can go inside," Danitia said, tugging Scarlet's arm. "Come on. Maybe the door isn't locked. Come on, guys. Let's check it out."

That's so like Danitia. Never likes to wait for anything.

I took a deep breath and followed them around the side of the house to the front. "Why would the door be locked?" Cheng said. "No one has lived here for a hundred years, right?"

"We'll soon find out," Danitia said.

Scarlet glanced back at me. She knew I wasn't ready to go into the mansion. As we approached the front stairs, I was the only one who was truly scared.

I kept checking my shadow as we walked. Would it start to change shape again?

The sun kept going in and out of the clouds. It made shadows play over the wide concrete steps that led up to the front doors. The double doors were tall and wide, the paint peeling and faded. The round, metal doorknobs were covered in a thick layer of rust.

I wished the doors had windows so I could look inside. But they were solid.

Danitia ran up the steps first. She raised her fist and pounded hard on a door.

"Are you crazy? Why did you knock?" Cheng demanded, hanging back on the top step.

Danitia grinned. "Just being polite."

I screamed as someone on the other side of the door knocked back.

"I *knew* it was haunted!" I cried.

13

Scarlet grabbed my arm. "Riley, what is your *problem*?"

"S-someone knocked—" I stammered.

She pointed to a tree hanging over the front of the house. A long branch tapped against the stone wall, swaying in the wind. *Knock knock knock.*

"Watch out! That tree is going to attack!" Carter cried.

Everyone laughed.

"It wasn't a tree branch," I insisted. "It came from the other side of the door." But I wasn't so sure. Maybe they were right about the branch. I looked up and watched it tap the wall.

Danitia wrapped her hand around a doorknob. I moved back. Toward the steps. I glanced to the street, ready to run.

This is a big mistake.

She twisted the knob. "Ouch. It's all rusty." She wiped her hand on the leg of her jeans. Then she grabbed the door again. And pushed.

The door didn't budge.

"It's stuck shut," Danitia said.

"Let's go," I said. "We're not supposed to be here."

Scarlet stepped up beside Danitia and tried the other door. They both groaned as they pushed as hard as they could.

"I don't think they're locked," Scarlet said. "I think they're just jammed."

"Maybe we should listen to Riley," Cheng said softly. "Maybe we should leave. It's getting late."

He was right. The afternoon sun was dipping low behind the trees. A blanket of shadows stretched across the front yard.

Carter turned to me. "You play the *Shudder Mansion* game all the time?"

I nodded.

"Well, when you play the game, how do you get through the front doors?"

"It's easy," I said. "You just slide right through them."

"Well, we can't slide through these," Carter said. "What's on the other side of the door, anyway?"

I pictured the opening scene of the game. "It's a wide, round, empty entryway," I said. "Very bare. Very high ceilings. It's like a big circle, and there are a lot of doors all around."

"And the doors lead to the rooms?" Carter asked.

I nodded. "The doors are all shut. They all have dangerous things behind them. All kinds of evil spirits and monsters and frightening creatures. You have to choose a door. Then you have to battle whatever is behind it."

Danitia was still twisting the doorknob. "That's no help," she said.

"Yeah, that's only a game," my sister agreed. "It's not going to help us at all."

"Let me try," Carter said. He shoved Danitia out of the way. "Boys are stronger than girls."

Danitia and Scarlet rolled their eyes. Carter lowered himself to one of the doorknobs. He wrapped both hands around it, took a deep breath, let out the breath with a groan—and heaved himself forward, pushing with all his strength.

Nothing moved. He tried to jerk the door back and forth, but his hands slid off the knob and he stumbled backward. I caught him before he toppled down the concrete steps.

"Thanks, Riley." He rubbed the rust off his hands on the front of my shirt. "We need to talk to Mrs. Blume," he said. "We need someone to come here and—"

Before Carter could finish his sentence, a loud, angry shout rang out. "Hey, what are you kids doing up there?" Someone stood at the street, half hidden in the shadow of the trees.

Was it a police officer?

Scarlet and Danitia leaped off the steps and took off running. Carter and Cheng followed, scrambling to the ground, then zigzagging through the trees.

No one said a word or made a sound. They just ran off silently, in all directions, heads lowered, backpacks bouncing on their backs.

Why did I linger in a corner of the front stoop? I had an idea. I hunched against the wall and stood perfectly still until the man in the street moved on.

I waited awhile to make sure he was gone. Then I slid my phone out of my jeans pocket.

My idea was to take some photos of the front and back of the mansion. I knew that if we survived our night in Shudder Mansion, we would have to make a report to Mrs. Blume. So I thought it would be a good idea to start out with photos of the house before we entered it.

I'll start a blog, I decided. *I'll add some photos to it every day.*

I'll try to tell the whole story of our Shudder Mansion adventure with photos.

I know what you're thinking. *I* was the one who wanted to get away from the old house as fast as I could. But now that I knew we weren't going inside . . . Now that I knew we *couldn't* get inside, I felt much braver.

It's a good idea, I thought. *I'll stay and take some early photos to use for our report. After all, I'm the expert on Shudder Mansion. I'm the one who plays the game and knows the stories. I'll probably be the one in our group in charge of the report to Mrs. Blume.*

I climbed off the stoop, backed up a bit, and took a few shots of the front windows. I bent down low and took a dramatic shot of the front steps, looking up to the double doors.

I turned and snapped a photo of the tall stone tower at the left side of the mansion. Then I backed up, took a few more photos of the front, looking through the trees.

Later, I'll shoot some videos for the blog, I decided. But for now, photos would do.

I was concentrating hard on my phone. I had it raised up to my face, studying the angles that I wanted to show of the front of the house . . . then . . .

"Aaaaaiiii!" I uttered a scream as a stabbing pain rocked my head and shot down my whole body.

Someone hit me.

Attacked! I've been attacked!

14

[faint mirrored text from previous page bleeding through]

Someone smashed my head.

I sank to my knees. The pain forced me to shut my eyes.

I waited for it to fade, but my head felt as if it might explode.

When I finally opened my eyes, I saw the thick tree branch above me. I realized I had walked right into it.

Not an attack. Not someone. Just a stupid tree branch.

I waited a while longer, taking long, deep breaths. Slowly, the pain stopped throbbing. The dizziness faded. I climbed back up to my feet.

I was gripping my phone so hard, my hand ached. I took a few more breaths and, still feeling shaky, gazed at the house.

One more shot. I wanted to do a close-up of the door and the two doorknobs.

The afternoon sun was low behind the tangle of trees now. Gray evening light washed over the house. The wind turned cooler, and my forehead still throbbed as I climbed back onto the stoop.

I stepped up to the front doors, my phone raised in front of me.

I was so focused on the shot, it took me a long while to see that *the doors were open!*

"Huh?" I cried out, and the phone nearly slipped from my hand. I jammed it into my jeans pocket and stared at the opening between the doors.

They were both just open a crack. I could see only a curtain of darkness behind them. I stared hard, my heart suddenly pounding in my chest.

When did the doors open?

Should I take a look inside?

A cold wind swirled around me, holding me in place. But it wasn't the wind that sent chills down my back. It was the sight of those open doors.

Had Scarlet and Danitia pulled them open without realizing it? Did Carter's big heave force them open?

Or were they opened by someone—or some*thing*—inside the creepy old mansion?

A cold feeling swept down my whole body.

I had no choice. After all the games I'd played, I *had* to slip through the doors and enter the old house. I *had* to look inside.

Was I scared? Three guesses. I told myself I'd just take a quick peek.

I reached out and grabbed the door on the right. Solid wood. Solid. This wasn't a game. This was the real Shudder Mansion, and here I was, pulling the heavy door, listening to it squeak and groan as I tugged it open.

I slipped inside—and uttered a startled gasp.

15

I blinked several times in disbelief. The entry-way was exactly the same as in the video game.

I stood on the edge of a tall, round room. Gray walls all around. Black tile floor. A crystal chandelier hanging from the high ceiling.

And, just as in the game, narrow doorways were cut into the round gray walls. Closed doorways. I counted eight of them.

I was still blinking. I guess I couldn't believe what I was seeing. I'd never been in this house, but it didn't feel that way. The real Shudder Mansion appeared just as it did in the game.

What was behind the doors? The same evil monsters as in the game?

I punched my fist against the cold stone wall. Solid. It was real. This definitely wasn't a game.

We can't spend a night in this place, I thought.

It's just too dangerous.

Maybe Mrs. Blume will let us spend a night at the zoo instead.

My eyes gazed at the circle of doors. Now that I was in the mansion, I couldn't decide what to do. One part of me wanted to turn and run back outside as fast as I could.

The other part of me wanted to do just a tiny bit of exploring.

I'll just look behind one door, I decided.

I picked one that was closest to me and turned the rusted doorknob. The door creaked but slid open easily.

I peered into a large, empty room. It might have been a living room at some time. Strange. I didn't remember seeing this room in the game. I took a careful step inside.

Tall windows across the room were caked with thick dust. But dull orange afternoon sunlight managed to push through. It formed a puddle of soft light on the bare wooden floor.

The air smelled musty and sour. The sunlight washed over a tangle of cobwebs on the wall to my right. They were like a thick curtain, stretching from floor to ceiling.

I took a step closer and saw *hundreds* of dead flies trapped in the ancient wall of webs. I squinted in disbelief—and saw a tiny skeleton caught in the thick gray strands. The skeleton of a mouse. It must have caught itself in the web and died there.

A shiver ran down my back. I turned away from the ugly cobweb curtain.

I found myself gazing at a large square mirror on the wall. The mirror rose over a stone fireplace that was heaped with ashes. The ashes were nearly as tall as me. Chunks of wood were broken off the mantel above the fireplace.

I moved toward the mirror. Like the windows, it was caked with dust. I squinted, trying to see myself—and gasped when I saw something move.

Something in the mirror. Someone moving behind me.

Holding my breath, I inched closer. And stared at the figure reflected in the mirror.

"Hey—!" I choked out. "Mia? What are *you* doing here?"

16

She didn't answer.

Her blond hair fluttered around her pale face, as if she were standing in a soft breeze. She wore the same white top and pale blue skirt as the day before.

I stared at her reflection. "Mia?"

I spun around to face her.

"Huh?"

She wasn't there.

"Mia?"

I started to breathe hard. My chest suddenly felt tight. I turned back to the mirror.

And there she was. Her dark eyes gazed out at me. She raised a hand to smooth down one side of her straight blond hair.

A tense laugh escaped my throat. "Are you playing a trick on me? How are you doing this?"

She smiled.

I spun around again to face her.

The room was empty. She wasn't there.

"Mia?" My voice came out in a hoarse croak.

I spun to the mirror. There was her reflection in the glass. I turned back to the room. No sign of her.

It had to be some kind of a trick. A simple trick. So why was my whole body tight with fright? Why was I gasping for breath?

I peered into the mirror. I gasped again as Mia gave me a smile and a wave. Then she turned and walked out of view.

"Mia? Mia? Are you here?" I managed to choke out.

But the room was empty. And now the mirror reflected only my bewildered face and the empty room and the darkening sunlight.

"I've got to get out of here," I said out loud. "I have to tell the others we can't stay here. We have to find another adventure. This place will give us nightmares for the rest of our lives."

I slipped through the open doorway, pulled the door shut behind me—and stopped. *Hey! What's going on?*

I expected to find myself back in the round front entryway with the circle of doors.

But I peered down a dark, narrow hallway. I took a few steps. My shoes slid on the dust, as thick as a carpet, that covered the floor. The hall stretched for a mile, with dark rooms on both sides all the way down.

Did I go out the wrong door?

I turned to go back into the room with the mirror. But the door behind me was gone.

"Whoa. Wait a minute."

I'd just stepped out the door. And now I saw solid wall. I stepped up to it and ran my hands over the wood. I gazed all around.

Definitely no door here.

I began to make my way slowly to the next door and the next. I knew there had to be a doorway that would lead to the outside.

I stopped when I heard a soft whining sound. A shrill cry. Somewhere behind me.

A cat?

The black cat I'd seen out in the yard?

I started to walk faster, but it was nearly dark as night in the narrow hall. I couldn't see where I was going. The cat's mournful cries followed me down the hall.

Finally, I spotted an open door near the end of the hall. I stepped into the doorway. Another room. I squinted into the darkness.

"Oh." I took a step back as a figure came into view. A skeleton. A human skeleton, lighted by dying sunlight from a window at the far wall.

The skeleton appeared to stand on its own in the center of the room. Its toothless grin was frozen on its eyeless skull. I saw thick spiderwebs clinging to its rib cage. Its legs were spread, knee bones slightly bent. Standing there.

Just standing there, bony arms hanging limply, nearly to the floor.

I stared into the gray light. I'd never seen a real skeleton before—not even at the museum. What was holding the bones together? How was it standing upright like that?

I didn't have much time to think about it. I heard a rattling sound—*and then the skeleton started to move!*

As I gaped in horror, it did a short dance. Like a sailor's jig.

Its bony feet tapped against the wooden floor, and its long arms bent in front of it and in back. It moved its arms and tapped its feet, and danced to a silent rhythm.

The skull tilted from side to side. Its jaw bounced up and down, making clicking sounds, as the bones did their dance.

And suddenly I remembered it.

I remembered the Dancing Skeleton from level one of the *Shudder Mansion* game.

Yes. I'd run into it in the game. The skeleton seemed harmless, just a grinning figure that wanted to dance.

But if you watched him too long, he would DANCE OVER YOU.

He would pull you to the floor and grind his hard, bony feet over your body.

He would kick and pound and dance on you till he flattened your bones.

I remembered the Dancing Skeleton. And I knew I should run. But I waited too long . . . too long . . .

He turned. He saw me and stopped his dance. He raised his long, bony arms to me. And he took a lurching dive.

With a sharp cry, I ducked out of his grasp. I spun away and started to run.

I tore blindly through the darkness, past the closed doors. Back down the hall, unable to see or breathe or think about anything but those rattling bones coming after me.

The cries of the cat rose higher and more shrill, drowning out the shaking bones. At the end of the hall, I saw a door with dim sunlight seeping through the bottom. I darted toward it.

I heard the clatter of bones close behind me. The sad cat wails. The bones . . . the bones . . . the snap of the jaw and the *thud* of the foot bones on the hard wood floor . . .

I was nearly to the door. A choking sound escaped my throat as I felt bony fingers, hard, bony fingers, wrap around my neck.

The skeleton grabbed me. Tugged me back. The fingers pressed hard into my skin. The eyeless head grinned at me with its toothless jaws hanging open.

"No—!" I tried to cry out. To squirm away.

But the skeleton held tight.

And began to dance with me in its painful grip.

Its bony knees bumped my legs. It shoved me and lifted me with surprising strength.

The skeleton was forcing me to dance.

Dance. Dance. We tapped the floor together. It gripped me in its powerful hold and pushed my legs. I had no choice. I had to dance with it.

The thud of my shoes on the floor. The clatter and snap of bones. Dancing. Dancing.

"Nooooooo!" I screamed—and yanked away.

I broke free from the dancing skeleton. And gasped when I saw what I gripped in my hand.

Finger bones. Two of its finger bones had ripped off into my hand.

"Oh, noooo," I groaned. I spun away. Out the front door. My chest nearly bursting. I couldn't breathe. I could only run.

I was running blindly. Everything a blur. A swirling, colorless blur.

And then the world went black.

I don't know for how long. The blackness hung over my eyes and pressed me down. Like a dark creature sitting on my chest. I couldn't move. Couldn't raise my arms or bend my legs.

And when I finally opened my eyes, it took me a few seconds to realize I was flat on my back on the ground. And I was staring up into a girl's face.

I was staring up at my sister.

"Scarlet? What are you doing here?"

17

"Are you okay? Riley, are you okay?" She placed her hands on my shoulders and gently shook me.

"I . . . don't know," I answered, my mouth dry as cotton.

She leaned over me, her hair falling around her face. "Oh, I was so worried."

I blinked up at her. "What's . . . happening?"

"I . . . I came back to look for you," Scarlet said. "You didn't run away when we did. I was worried. I came back. And I saw something in the grass under this tree." She pointed up at a low tree branch above us.

"I thought it was a pile of clothes or something," she continued. "But I walked closer—and I saw that it was *you*. You were flat on your back with your eyes closed."

She pressed her hands to her cheeks. Her eyes grew wide. "I . . . I didn't know if you were alive. I mean . . . you didn't move. I guess you were out cold."

I gazed up at the tree branch. I tried to raise my head. But a stab of pain forced me to lie back down.

"I made sure you were breathing," Scarlet said. "I was so . . . relieved. But then I didn't know what to do." She rubbed two fingers over my forehead. "Riley, you have a big red bruise there."

And then it all came clear to me. "I was taking photos, then I ran into the tree branch," I told her. "It must have knocked me out. I wonder how long I've been lying here."

"I'm so glad I came back," Scarlet said. Her whole body shuddered. "That was scary."

Scary? Yes.

I pictured Mia's reflection in the mirror. The thick curtain of cobwebs filled with dead flies. I heard the cat cries, so shrill in my ears. The tap and jangle of the skeleton bones as the Dancing Skeleton came after me.

All a dream?

All of it only in my mind? Was I passed out here on the grass the whole time?

The terrifying pictures were still clear and real. My fear lingered in my chest.

A tree branch. A tree branch had knocked me out. And I had that frightening nightmare about being in Shudder Mansion.

I rubbed a finger over the bruise on my forehead. The pain had faded a little. I raised my head slowly and turned my gaze to the front of the house.

I focused on the doors above the front steps. They were shut. The windows on both sides of the front stoop reflected the late afternoon sun.

Scarlet stood up and reached both hands down to me. "Can I help you up?"

I lifted both arms.

Whoa. Wait.

Something strange. I was gripping something tightly in my right hand.

With a groan, I lifted my head. I opened my hand and stared. Stared at the two finger bones gripped tightly in my palm.

SLAPPY HERE, EVERYONE.

Haha. Riley seems a little confused. Was he inside the mansion? Or was he taking a snooze in the grass?

This story has *everything*—mystery, suspense, thrills. There's just one thing missing—ME! I make every story a *scream*! Ha ha.

If I lived in Shudder Mansion, I'd enjoy being there. I wouldn't need any electricity—because *I light up every room!* Ha.

Did you know my nickname is *Sunshine*?

Did you also know that I lie a lot? Hahaha.

I know what you're all waiting for. You're waiting for Riley and Scarlet and their friends to go spend the night in Shudder Mansion. You're waiting for the *real* scares to begin.

Will they survive?

I hope not.

I *hate* a happy ending! Hahahaha!

18

I grabbed the car door handle as Dad pulled to the curb at the side of Shudder Mansion. Mom turned around in the passenger seat. "Riley—don't jump out before the car stops," she said.

Scarlet laughed. "He can't wait to go inside and start screaming."

I shoved her shoulder. "I'm not going to scream," I said. "*You* will be the one calling for help."

"You both have a bad attitude," Dad said, shutting down the engine and tucking the car key into his jacket pocket. "It may be a long, scary night. We're all going to have to *help* each other."

"Sure," Scarlet said. "I'll help him cry like a baby and run for his life."

Not funny.

We climbed out of the car. It was a chilly, damp night. Low clouds blocked the stars and the moon. A sharp wind shook the trees and the tall weeds in the Shudder Mansion yard.

I shivered in the sudden cold.

Scarlet laughed. "See? He's shivering already!"

"Just from the cold," I said. "I'm not scared, Scarlet. I've played the *Shudder Mansion* game a thousand times. The game is a lot scarier than what will happen to us tonight."

I wish I believed that.

Actually, I didn't know what to think. I'd tossed the skeleton fingers into the trees, but I couldn't stop thinking about them.

I would never admit it to Scarlet, but I'd never been so terrified in my life. None of my friends knew it—but I had gone to Mrs. Blume and begged her to change the assignment. I told her the old mansion wasn't safe.

"Your friends all want to do it," she said. "And remember, your parents will be there. You're going to make a great video. And you'll have fun, Riley."

Fun?

Well . . . here we were. Ready to have "fun."

"Don't forget the cooler," Mom said. "We brought a lot of drinks and snacks for everyone."

Dad lifted a tall plastic spray bottle from the back of the car. "And hand cleaner. You'll need plenty of hand cleaner. There have to be a lot of germs in this old place."

Both of my parents are fanatics about hand cleaner. Every time you look at them, they're squirting their palms. They must have the oiliest hands in town.

Behind us, a long SUV pulled up to the curb. Carter climbed out, followed by his housekeeper. He had told everyone his parents were in France. So his housekeeper came instead. She and Carter moved to the back of the SUV and began pulling out all the electronic equipment Carter had promised to bring.

"Hey, Riley!" Carter shouted. He raised a small camcorder in one hand. "This is the GoPro I used on our safari in Kenya. I'll show you how to use it. It's not that complicated. Even you can handle it. We can both take some video tonight."

"Awesome," I said. I knew Carter wouldn't stop bragging and showing off about how much cool stuff he had and how he was so much smarter than the rest of us. So, why fight him?

By eight o'clock, the whole team was gathered in the front entryway. We opened the doors that circled the hall. No monsters lurking behind any of them.

I breathed a sigh of relief. In the game, I always hated having to open one of the doors, knowing that I'd be attacked.

I led the way through a door on the left into a large square room that could have once been a dining room. We piled our jackets against one wall. Some of the parents began lighting candles and setting them up around us. Most everyone was talking at once, and our voices echoed off the high stone walls.

I gazed around the room, taking a count of how many we were. I'm not sure why I did it. It just seemed like a good way to start the night.

Carter was fiddling with his camcorder while his housekeeper dragged a bunch of other equipment into the hall. Scarlet and Danitia were laughing about something and bumping knuckles.

Cheng explained that his parents work at night. So he brought his grandparents. They were both gray-haired, short, and thin, dressed in black. They kept smiles on their faces but didn't speak.

Danitia's parents were as enthusiastic as she was. They were greeting everyone, passing out bags of chips and pretzels and helping carry the candles down the hall, chattering the whole time about how exciting this was.

And then I blinked when someone else walked into the room. Mia.

What was *she* doing here?

19

Scarlet and Mia greeted each other like old friends. Mia wore a heavy black sweater that came down nearly to her knees. Her blond hair was tied back behind her head.

Carter looked up from his machine. "Hey, hi. You don't go to our school," he said. "Who are you?"

"Her name is Mia, and she's my friend," Scarlet answered him. "I invited her. She doesn't know anyone, and I thought she'd have fun."

"Hope everyone doesn't mind," Mia said shyly.

I stared at her, thinking about her reflection in the mirror. Thinking about that afternoon we met when I suddenly could see her skull underneath her skin.

She's trouble, I thought. I felt a chill at the back of my neck. *I know there's something strange about her.*

"Are your parents here?" Scarlet asked Mia.

"They're coming later," Mia replied.

My dad began to clap his hands together and shouted, "Quiet, everyone. Can we have it quiet? We have a plan."

It took a little while for everyone to settle down. Mom and Dad both stepped into the center of the room. Their faces appeared to flicker in and out in the candlelight. The whole room pulsed dark, then light as the candle flames trembled.

"We parents got together earlier this week and made a plan," Dad announced. "You guys are going to have a lot of fun tonight."

Fun? I thought. *Will it be fun?*

"Now here's our plan," Dad said.

Scarlet and I exchanged glances. Neither of them had bothered to tell *us* anything about a plan. Why was it a big secret?

Carter had his camcorder trained on my parents. He was recording every word.

"We adults are going to stay downstairs," Mom said. "This room will be our headquarters."

"We'll have all the drinks and snacks down here," Dad continued. "We have lit up the second floor for you. There are candles and a few lanterns hung on the walls."

"And we'll be down here for you," Danitia's mom chimed in. "If we hear you screaming for help, we'll come running. Otherwise, you're on your own up there for any adventure you can find."

"Riley, where do we go?" Scarlet asked.

I pointed to the stairway at the back of the room. "That way. Up to the second floor," I said.

It also leads to a rabid two-headed hyena that can bite your head off from the front and from behind at the same time, I remembered.

"Better let me go first," I said, my hands shaking. I grabbed two of Carter's light poles that he brought to help light up the place. I led the way to the stairs. "If a hyena attacks, I can fight it off with these poles."

Everyone laughed.

They thought I was making a joke.

"Maybe Bigfoot is up there," Scarlet said. "We could get him on our video."

"You're not funny," I said. "I'm just telling you what's in the game."

Carter had brought so much equipment, everyone had to help carry it upstairs.

Our parents were all wishing us good luck and making jokes as we started the steep climb. None of them were taking the danger seriously. I guess I couldn't blame them. None of them had ever played the game.

The old wooden stairs creaked under our shoes. One floorboard was missing, and I nearly tripped and fell into the hole. I grabbed for the banister, and a chunk of it broke off in my hand.

Scarlet and Mia were right behind me. "Riley, are you a total klutz in the game, too?" my sister said.

Mia chuckled.

"Scarlet, you're a riot," I muttered.

The air grew colder as we climbed. A burst of wind greeted us near the top. The air smelled musty, sour.

"Evil spirits like to stay up high," I heard Carter telling Danitia. "They don't like to be near the ground."

Danitia let out a tense laugh. "So you think it's more dangerous on the second floor?"

"Definitely."

Since when is Carter the evil spirits expert? I wondered.

I paused at the top of the stairs and glanced around. Every muscle in my body tensed. I'd fought the monstrous hyena several times. Sometimes I won. Sometimes I died.

No sign of the deadly creature.

I saw a wide room with windows all around. A long wooden table stood in the middle. Half a dozen candles burned brightly on the table. And a flaming torch was hung on one wall.

A narrow door in the back wall stood half-open. Maybe a closet door? I could see only darkness behind it.

Shoes scuffled over the wooden floor as everyone stepped into the room. "At least it's nice and bright up here," Cheng said. "Not exactly cozy, but . . ." His voice trailed off.

"I'll set up my equipment over there," Carter said. He pointed to the wall across from the stairway. "Careful with the motion detector. It's very delicate. Don't drop anything. This stuff cost a fortune!"

Danitia, Cheng, and Mia obediently dragged the cases and screens and electronic devices to the wall.

"Okay, everyone stand back," Carter said, waving both hands as if shooing away a dog. "I have to set this up myself. Stay back. I'm the only one with the skill and the knowledge to get this equipment to work."

Nice guy, isn't he?

"What is all this equipment supposed to do?" Scarlet asked.

"Detect evil spirits, of course," Carter snapped.

"I just thought of something," my sister said.

Everyone stopped to listen.

"Where are you going to plug this stuff in, Carter? There's no electricity."

Danitia groaned and slapped her forehead. "Oh, wow. *Now* she thinks of it!"

Cheng shook his head. "We lugged this stuff up here for *nothing*?"

Carter raised a finger to his lips. "Shut up, everyone. Everyone, chill. I'm a pro, remember? I brought my own generator."

He dragged a large square box across the room. "This will power all the equipment. It runs on gasoline," he explained. "We plug everything into it. Then I start it by pulling this rope, like a lawn mower."

We stood and watched Carter as he went to work. What else could we do? He wouldn't let us help.

It took a long time to get all the devices and machines set up and plugged in. All the while, I stayed tense and alert. Watching for any creatures that might attack. And watching Mia. She stayed close to Scarlet and hardly spoke.

But I didn't trust her. And I still couldn't believe Scarlet had invited her.

"Stand back. Here we go," Carter said, motioning us all away again. He stepped up to the generator and gave the rope a strong, two-handed pull. The generator made a chugging sound and started to roar. The lights Carter brought came on. The video screens clicked and flashed into motion.

Carter took a bow. We all applauded. It's so annoying how Carter always needs to hog the spotlight and be the star. But I had to admit this was pretty awesome.

I grabbed the GoPro camera and started to take a video of all the equipment humming away. Scarlet and Mia sat down cross-legged on the floor in front of the motion detector screen.

Cheng and Danitia stood behind them. They waved to the camera as I panned it past him.

The generator worked fine for about three minutes.

Then a deafening explosion made me jump.

The lights flickered and died. The screens went dark. I gasped as a flash of fiery light burst from the generator, followed by a sizzling current sound. Then silence.

I stood gazing at the dead equipment, breathing hard. And a powerful gust of cold wind swirled in from out of nowhere.

The torch on the wall made a loud *whoooosh* as it died. The red flames turned purple, then went dark.

All the candles went out.

All of them. All at once.

"Oh, wow," I muttered, blinking into the complete blackness. "I don't believe this."

"I can't see a thing!" Cheng cried.

"Somebody, do something!" Danitia shouted.

I gazed into the inky darkness. No light at all. Not a flicker.

I took a step toward the others, then stopped.

Something plopped heavily onto my foot.

I tried to kick it off. But I felt it slide under my jeans cuff.

Something . . . something warm and soft . . . with scratchy, prickly feet . . . something *alive* was crawling up my leg.

91

20

I screamed and started to kick my leg.

Prickly feet dug into the skin on my calf as the creature crawled higher.

I slapped at it. Twisted and kicked.

"Riley? What's wrong?" I heard Scarlet's cry in the dark.

"What's going on?" Cheng demanded. "What's happening?"

I grabbed at the creature under my jeans. I could feel it. A soft lump.

Moaning, I gave another hard kick. I felt it slide down my leg. I heard a *thummmp* as it hit the floor.

I cried out and shielded my eyes as a bright beam of light shone on my face. Squinting, I followed the light as it slid over the floor.

"How smart was I to bring this LED flashlight?" Carter said.

He shone the light on the creature. It was a

mouse. It stood on its hind legs, staring up at me, its head tilted to one side.

"That's a big mouse!" Danitia cried.

"It . . . climbed up my leg," I stammered.

But then I recognized it. Suddenly, I remembered it from the game.

It wasn't an ordinary mouse.

"We've got to get *out* of here!" I cried.

"Riley, it's just a mouse," Carter said.

"N-no," I stammered.

I didn't have to say anything else. In the light from Carter's flashlight, we all saw the creature begin to grow.

Standing on its hind legs, it grew quickly. Stretched and grew. In seconds, it was the size of a cat. Its bones creaked and cracked as it rose up, stretched, rolling its eyes, cranking its head from side to side. As I stared in horror, it rose to the size of a German shepherd!

It gnashed its pointed teeth. The click of its jaws echoed off the walls. It swiped giant paws in the air, preparing to attack. A raspy growl escaped its open mouth.

And we took off.

I reached the doorway first and tore into the pitch black hall.

I hesitated. Which way to run? Which way?

It didn't matter. We just had to get away from the jaws of the mouse monster.

Running in darkness, my shoes thudding on the hard floor, I heard the others behind me. Heard them breathing hard and murmuring their fear, sharp cries and whimpers. And I listened for the heavy *bump* of giant mouse paws as the creature chased after us, its prey.

Unable to see, my head smacked a wall. We'd come to the end of the hall. I let out a groan and staggered back, fighting off the pain and dizziness.

We all huddled in this dark corner. Carter's white beam of light danced over us, revealing the terror on our faces.

"We can't stay here," I said. "This was a terrible idea. The house is just like the video game. The same creatures live here. They're all deadly. All of them."

"It can't be the same," Mia said. "That's crazy."

"You saw that mouse!" I cried. "How crazy was *that*?"

"We . . . we thought the old house was deserted. Empty." Carter shook his head.

"Well, it's not," I said. "The game is *true*. That giant mouse is only on level two. If we run into more dangerous creatures . . . If we run into *The Beast* . . . we're doomed."

"The Beast?" Cheng asked in a tiny voice. "What's *that*?"

I heard sounds down the hall. Thumps and

scrapes. "No time to talk," I said. "We have to find our parents and get out of here."

"But . . . how do we get out?" Scarlet demanded.

Before I could answer, I saw a flash of light from a wall torch down the hall. An enormous creature burst into the light—and I opened my mouth in a scream of horror.

"It's too late," I told them, watching the creature lumber toward us. "It's the Beast."

21

"Hurry! This way!" I choked out.

We hurtled down the hall. Turned. Tore through another hall.

I had no time to tell them that the Beast was the most deadly creature of Shudder Mansion. Sometimes human, sometimes an enormous roaring animal, it couldn't be defeated.

When I played the game, I never even tried to face the Beast. I turned and ran. I knew if I tried to battle him, it would be *Game Over* for me.

But this wasn't the game. The Beast was real. All of the horrors of the *Shudder Mansion* game were real. My friends and I weren't having a silly, safe adventure we could video. We were in real-life danger we probably wouldn't survive.

Carter's light danced over the floor and walls ahead of us as we ran. Not too far behind us, I could hear the grunts and growls and heavy footsteps of the creature pursuing us.

"We can't keep running," I said. "We have to find a place to hide."

"That door is open," Cheng said, pointing to a dark opening just ahead of us.

"Be careful," I warned. "The Beast is very clever. He likes to set traps."

But we didn't have time to be careful. We dove into the room, gasping for breath, holding our sides.

Carter's light swept all around. The room appeared to be a kitchen.

Danitia groaned and held her nose. "Ewwwww. Stinks in here," she said.

The sour aroma choked my throat. "Like rotting, decayed meat or something," I said, breathing out.

Scarlet pointed. "What's that pile of stuff on the kitchen counter? Are those animal skeletons?"

Before anyone could answer, I uttered a startled cry. "Hey—my shoes—!"

Everyone discovered it at the same time.

The floor was soft and sticky. My shoes were stuck in some kind of gunk.

I struggled to raise my foot. I couldn't lift my shoe out of the thick, sticky goo. I stood there on one foot for a while, trying to decide what to do.

The others were struggling, too. "Can't walk," Cheng groaned, bending his knees. His arms bobbed at his sides as he tried to keep his balance. He looked like he was doing a high-wire act in the circus.

I saw Danitia grab the back of one knee, trying to pry her foot out of the thick muck on the floor. She pulled hard—stumbled forward—and fell facedown with a horrified scream.

"Oooh, it smells! It smells!" Danitia cried, down on the floor. "Help me! Somebody!"

Scarlet and Mia struggled over to her and reached to pull her up from the sticky mess. We all were trying to pull our shoes free, tilting and squirming to keep our balance. The light from Carter's flashlight zigzagged over the ceiling as he struggled to walk.

"We're like flies in a spiderweb," Danitia said. "We can't move at all. What can we do?"

"It's a trap," I said, shaking my head sadly. "The Beast set a trap for us—and we walked right into it."

"Now what?" Cheng asked in a trembling voice. "What happens in the game?"

"He'll eat us one by one."

22

Scarlet grabbed my arm. "Help me. Can you pull me to the door?"

I twisted to reach her—and my foot came out of my sneaker. With a cry of surprise, I gazed down at my shoe, stuck in the syrupy gunk. "I can't move . . ." I rasped, trying to balance on one foot.

I can't stand like this much longer, I thought, teetering to one side. I started to panic—and then it came to me.

I had been in this trap once before. Yes, I knew how we could escape—if the Beast didn't get to us first.

"Take off your shoes," I said.

The idea did not go over well.

"No way!"

"Are you crazy?"

"If we do that, our *socks* will be stuck in the goo."

"That's totally stupid."

99

"Take off your shoes and socks," I said. "Leave them where they are. Listen to me. I beat this trap once. I know this will work."

"But then our *feet* will be stuck," Danitia said. "The only way out of here is to *fly*."

"Listen, everyone, you've got to believe me—" I said.

"What if we all hold on to each other?" Cheng suggested. "If we move as a group, maybe we can pull each other to the door."

"We have to call our parents," Scarlet said. "We need them to help us—"

"I already checked my phone. There's no cell service," I said. "And even if we all shouted at once, no way they'd hear us. Besides, they wouldn't get here in time." My voice trembled. "The Beast is right down the hall."

Carter twisted and bent in the goo. He looked like he was doing a strange dance. "I . . . can't . . . budge," he said, gasping for breath. "Let's listen to Riley."

Whoa. That was a surprise.

"Okay. Take off your shoes and socks," I said. "Don't worry about stepping in the goo with your bare feet. The goo doesn't stick to human skin. You won't sink into it, I promise."

"That's crazy," Cheng muttered.

"This is *all* crazy," Danitia said.

"Riley is right. We'd better hurry," Mia said.

She had been silent this whole time. I'd almost forgotten she was there.

"I can't believe we're not getting this on the video," Carter muttered. "Mrs. Blume will never believe it."

"Hurry," I said. "Forget about the video. We're in a real trap. We're helpless in here. Hurry!"

I already had one shoe off. I put one hand on the wall to balance myself, leaned over, and pulled off the sock. I tossed the sock into the gunk.

Then I slid my foot out of my other shoe. I pulled off my sock, balled it up, and heaved it away.

I glanced around. I was the first one to take my shoes and socks off. All eyes were on me now.

"Check it out," I said. I was standing in the thick goo.

"My feet will bounce over the layer of gunk," I said. "They won't sink. They won't stick. And I'll be able to walk out of here without a problem."

I was standing on top of my shoes. Now I lifted my right foot and lowered it to the goo. Then, balancing carefully, I lowered my left foot into the sticky gunk.

They sank deep into the goo.

I tried to move. I couldn't pull them up. Both feet stuck.

A startled cry escaped my throat. "It . . . It didn't work," I stammered.

23

Everyone groaned.

"I knew it!" Scarlet cried.

And then I felt a tickle on the bottoms of my feet. The tickle became a push. I glanced down. It took a few seconds to realize what was happening.

The goo was pushing my feet up, bouncing them up to the surface.

I took a step. Then another.

Yes!

"I did it!" I shouted. "I'm free!"

The goo felt like Jell-O under my feet. But I walked over it until I reached the door. I poked my head out into the dark hall and peered both ways.

No sign of the Beast.

"Hurry!" I shouted.

"But what about our shoes?" Cheng demanded. "We can't walk around barefoot."

"Just leave them," I said. "It's better than being eaten by a monster."

I watched them scramble out of their shoes and socks. A few seconds later, we were huddled barefoot in the hall.

"We have to tell our parents what happened," Danitia said. "Maybe they can help us get our shoes back."

"Forget the shoes," I said. "Don't you understand the danger we're in? We have to get out of this house."

"He's right. But first we have to get the camcorder," Carter said. "We have to get this on video. We have to get *proof.*"

"We're going to die," I moaned. "We can't go back. We're going to die."

Carter ignored me. So did everyone else. They followed Carter back to the room, stumbling and fumbling in the dark. I'd never been so tense or alert in my life. With every footstep, I listened for sounds of the Beast or a glimpse of the hideous creature.

"I can't see a thing," Carter said. "Where is the camcorder? I've got to find my night vision goggles."

Outside the windows, low clouds had covered the moon. Dim gray light managed to seep in.

"Carter, do you still have those matches?" I asked. "Let's light some candles."

"My feet are freezing," Cheng said. "And I think I got a splinter walking down the hall."

We managed to light three or four candles. The soft glow brought the room into focus.

Carter picked up the GoPro camera and handed it to me. "Riley, let's video me talking about what happened in the room with the goo on the floor. Maybe we can go back there and take some shots of our shoes stuck in the floor."

"Go back there? No way!" Cheng and Danitia exclaimed in unison.

"Are you crazy?" I cried. "Didn't you hear what I said about the Beast? About this old house? It's deadly, Carter. There are monsters around every corner. And this isn't a game. It's real. We really could die."

Carter took a step back. For the first time, his grin faded and I saw a flash of fear on his face.

"Let's go," I said. "Now. No more talk till we are out of here and safe."

I took a few steps, but Danitia pulled me back. "What's your problem?" I snapped.

"Just wait a minute," Danitia said. "Wait a minute, everyone. Where is Scarlet?"

"Huh?" Her question sent a chill to the back of my neck. "Scarlet?"

I gazed around the room. I didn't see my sister.

"Did she escape the goo with us?" Mia asked.

"I . . . I don't know," Danitia said. "I think so. I think she was right behind me."

"Hey—Scarlet!" I shouted. My voice came out high and shrill. "Scarlet—are you here?"

No answer.

24

I froze. I had to force myself to breathe.

I grabbed a candle and darted out into the hall. "Scarlet! Scarlet?" I shouted her name again and again, listening to my voice ring off the dark walls.

Trying to shield the candle flame with one hand, I went running full speed back down the hall. My heartbeats thudded as loudly as my bare feet on the floorboards.

"Riley—where are you going?" I heard Cheng's voice behind me.

"To ... find ... Scarlet." I said.

As I ran, I tried to think. *Did anyone just vanish from sight in the video game? Did anyone just disappear?*

There were so many levels in the game. Some single player. Some multiplayer. The higher levels got more and more dangerous. And sometimes, when someone disappeared, they NEVER RETURNED.

I reached the room with the sticky floor. My chest felt about to burst. My head throbbed.

"Scarlet? Are you in here?"

I pushed the candle in front of me. Raised it high so that its dim, flickering light spread over the floor.

I could see the shoes and socks, still sunk in the thick carpet of goo. No sign of my sister.

"Scarlet! Where *are* you?"

I turned and ran back to the others. My feet pounded the hard floor, but I didn't feel anything. I was numb now. Numb with fright.

The others greeted me with wide-eyed, frightened expressions on their faces. "You . . . didn't find her?" Mia stammered.

I shook my head. "Come on. We have to hurry downstairs. We have to tell our parents Scarlet has disappeared."

I started toward the stairs. Danitia and Cheng were close behind me.

We stopped when we heard shouts. Faint shouts.

I turned back into the room. I saw flashing lights outside the windows. Voices from outside.

"What's going on?" I cried.

We stampeded to the windows. Carter reached them first. He peered down to the lawn. "Our parents—!" he cried.

I pushed up beside him and squinted into the darting lights down below us. "Hey—!" I uttered a cry when I saw Mom and Dad. They were running across the grass.

I could hear them screaming. I could hear the other parents screaming, too, as they bolted toward the street. Danitia's parents outran my parents, as if it was a race to get away. Their jackets were flapping behind them.

Cheng's grandparents were far behind the others. But they were doing their best to run, holding hands as they hobbled awkwardly across the grass and tall weeds.

"They're running away!" I cried. "They're all running away!"

I pounded frantically on the window glass, pounded with both fists. "Stop!" I screamed at the top of my lungs. "Stop! Where are you going? Why are you leaving us here? Stop! Hey—*stop!*"

They couldn't hear me. The other kids were pounding on the window, too. Shouting and pounding.

But our terrified parents didn't turn back. Leaning forward into the wind, pumping their hands at their sides, they raced to the street, ran to their cars.

We grew silent. We stopped pounding the windows. We gave up.

Gave up . . . and watched them all drive away.

25

I covered my face with my hands. "I . . . don't . . . believe . . . it," I whispered.

"They all looked totally freaked," Carter said. "Like something scared them to death."

I pulled out my phone. "Maybe our phones will work in this part of the house. I'll try calling them. I'll find out what happened," I said.

Danitia already had her phone pressed to her ear. Carter pulled a phone from his jeans pocket.

I pushed my mom's number and waited.

Silence.

"Come on. Come on," I urged. I couldn't get the picture out of my mind, the picture of them running across the yard, screaming as they ran.

What scared them like that?

What was so frightening that they abandoned us?

"My phone isn't working." Danitia's trembling voice cut into my thoughts.

"Huh?" I lowered the phone from my ear and squinted at it. She was right. No bars in this part of the house, either. No service.

"We can't call them," Carter said, sighing. "We can't call out."

But then I heard a voice on my phone. A deep voice. "Hello?"

"Dad!" I cried. "Dad—what happened? Why did you leave? Why did everyone run out of here?"

Silence.

A long pause.

And then the laughter started. Deep, cold laughter. Evil laughter that rose higher and higher and grew louder.

I gazed at my friends. Everyone heard it.

The phone slipped from my hand. I caught it before it hit the floor. I raised it back to my ear.

"Who is this?" I screamed. "Who *is* this?"

I stared at the screen. No bars. The phone couldn't make a call.

Then who was laughing like that?

I held the phone in front of me—and heard the booming voice: "ARE YOU READY TO FEED THE BEAST?"

26

"We have to get out of here," I said. "We have to get help. We have to get help to find Scarlet."

No one replied. I could see by their faces that they were too frightened to move. I knew the terrifying voice of the Beast was in everyone's ears.

"We can run to my house," I said. "It's only two blocks away."

Gripping the candle in front of me, I ran out of the room and to the stairway. The wooden steps felt rough under my bare feet. But I didn't care. I had to get to Mom and Dad. I had to tell them about Scarlet.

The other kids came scrambling down the stairs after me. Candles burned all around the room, just as when we had gone upstairs. The snacks were still there, bags of chips and pretzels, and pizza slices spread out on a table. Cans of soda and water. Everything was as we left it—except the room was empty.

I ran into the entryway and stumbled over a crack in one of the tiles. Pain shot up my leg. I caught my balance against the double front doors. "Let's go!" I shouted. "We're outta here!"

I grabbed the doorknob on the right, twisted it, and pulled. The door didn't budge. I tried again. Nothing doing.

It was stuck shut. I grabbed the other doorknob in both hands—and pulled as hard as I could.

"Owww." Pain roared down my shoulder and side. The door didn't open.

"Let me try it," Carter said, shoving me out of the way.

He grabbed both knobs and pulled. Then he tried *pushing* the doors. Finally, he gave up with a groan. When he turned back to us, his face had gone pale and his chin trembled.

"Are we locked in?" he murmured. "Our parents wouldn't lock us in—*would* they?"

27

We all burst out talking at once, our voices shrill and frantic.

"Why would they do that?"

"They wouldn't lock us in. That's impossible."

"There are other doors. We have to try them."

"Our parents would never run out of here and lock the doors behind them."

"Then who locked them?"

"Shut up. Everyone shut up. If we're going to get out of here, we have to stay calm!" I shouted.

"How can we stay calm?" Cheng cried. "There's a terrifying monster in here. Watching us . . . Waiting for us . . ."

I shut my eyes and pictured the layout of the mansion. "There are two side doors. Sliding doors in one of the master bedrooms. A hidden door you can reach from the basement . . . " I said, thinking hard.

I opened my eyes. Cheng was tapping my shoulder. "Riley . . . Riley . . . ?"

I pushed his hand away. "What is it? I'm trying to picture the other doors."

Cheng motioned around the entryway. "Riley, where is Mia? Do you see Mia?"

Danitia gasped. Carter let out a cry.

I turned and gazed all around. "She's gone, too?"

The four of us shouted her name. No reply.

"One by one," Cheng muttered, shaking his head. "How is this happening? We're disappearing one by one. Did the Beast grab Scarlet and Mia?"

The three of them were staring at me, as if I had the answer. "I . . . I don't know what's happening," I stammered. "This isn't in the video game."

Danitia hugged herself tight to stop the trembling chills that shook her body. Tears formed in her eyes and rolled down her cheeks. "This . . . can't be happening."

Cheng was bent over, breathing hard, his mouth open, hands pressed on his knees. "I . . . I think I'm going to be sick," he said in a hoarse whisper.

"No. Keep it together," I said. "Please, everyone, keep it together."

"Riley, help us," Carter said softly. "You know this place from the game. Help us out of here."

Again, I pictured the layout of the mansion.

I'd been through the halls, through the rooms, battling evil spirits, fighting ghostly monsters of all kinds.

"Follow me," I said. "I can find a door. I know we can get out of here."

Boy, was I wrong.

28

We shielded our candles with our hands as we turned and started to make our way down the hall that led to the back of the house. The trembling orange candlelight guided our way through the deep darkness.

Fighting back my panic, I peered into every room we passed. Perhaps a window would be our way to escape.

But no. Some of the windows had bars over them. Some were boarded up. Others were too high on the wall for us to reach.

I led the way down the twisting halls. I thought I knew where I was going. So far, the house matched the game in every way. We passed a large den. I stopped to look at the pool table. Something tall and mossy had grown in the center of the table. Like a shrub. Or was it mold?

A sour aroma floated off the ugly growth. And

even in the dim light, I could see dozens of fat black insects crawling over it.

With a shudder, I turned away. My bare feet were frozen and were starting to tingle with a numb feeling. We turned the corner and stepped into another narrow hall.

"Scarlet? Scarlet? Can you hear me?"

My voice echoed as if in a tunnel.

No reply.

I couldn't stop the waves of panic rolling down my body. *Where can she be? Did the Beast or one of the other Shudder Mansion creatures take Scarlet and Mia and hide them somewhere? Or worse?*

A solid wood doorway—the back door—was just where I expected it to be. I had used it to escape several times while playing the *Shudder Mansion* game.

The others gathered around as I raised my candle to the door. "Oh, wow," I murmured as I saw the black metal bolt across the door. The bolt had a chain and a big padlock on one end.

I tugged at the padlock. It wouldn't budge.

"This door is locked, too," Cheng said in a tiny voice. His candle trembled in front of him.

"I should have brought my toolbox," Carter said. "I have a bolt cutter that would cut right through that one."

I wanted to slump onto the floor and cover

my head and wish this whole night away. But I knew I couldn't give up. I had to get help to find my sister. I had to get us out of this terrifying house.

"Wait! There's another back door," I remembered. I took off, trotting down the long hall to my right.

"I can't feel my feet," Danitia called. "Seriously. I think I have frostbite."

"Riley, don't run so fast," Cheng called. "I . . . can't keep up with you."

I turned back and saw him thumping along barefoot, limping, halfway down the hall. "Almost there," I called. "We'll be okay as soon as we get out of here."

"Oh, nooo," I moaned. The other back door was locked and bolted, too.

We all stared at the big padlock chained to the bolt.

"Well . . . we wanted adventure . . ." Carter murmured.

"We can't give up," Danitia said. "We have to get help."

"My grandparents must be worried about me already," Cheng said.

"Our parents ran off screaming," I said. "They haven't come back to see if we're okay. It's crazy. It's like they don't care."

"Something frightened them," Danitia said. "Something frightened them really badly."

"So why haven't they come back to rescue us?" I said.

I heard a sound. I raised my hand to silence the others.

A voice. A muffled voice. Very far away?

I spun away from the door and crossed to the middle of the hall. "Did you hear it, too?" I demanded, listening hard. "Did you hear something?"

"A voice?" Danitia said. "I think . . ."

I took off, running toward the sound. My heart started to pound in my chest. I stopped in front of a closed door at the end of the hallway and tugged it open. The others ran up beside me. Their candles sent a pale wash of light into the doorway.

I stared at the steps that led down. "The basement," I murmured. "Here it is." I moved onto the first step.

Danitia pulled me back. "Riley, we can't go down there. It's scary enough up here."

"She's right," Cheng said. "We have to find a way out. We can't go down there and . . ."

I pulled free of Danitia's hand and moved back into the stairwell. I cupped my hands around my mouth and shouted down in a breathless voice. "Scarlet? Are you down there? Mia? Scarlet? Can you hear me?"

Silence.

The four of us froze. No one moved.

"Scarlet? Can you hear me?"

And then I gasped as a hoarse, raspy voice sent up a reply. "Help me. Please—help me!"

"Scarlet?" I cried. "Is it you?"

"Help me." Yes. I recognized her voice. Yes. Yes. We'd found her.

"Please—help me!" she cried. "Hurry!"

29

I stumbled on the last step and landed hard on a concrete floor. Blinking in the darkness, I saw pale light through a wide window high on the far wall.

The air down here was hot and dry. One side of the room had a wall of wooden crates piled high from the floor to the ceiling.

"Ewww. What's that?" Danitia lowered her candle, and we gazed at the pale yellow bones of an animal skeleton stretched out in front of us. "I . . . I think . . . it's a rat," she stammered.

"An ex-rat," Carter said.

"Scarlet?" I shouted. I choked on the heavy, dry air. "Scarlet? Where are you?"

"Help me, Riley!" her shrill, frightened voice rang out. "Hurry!"

Kicking up a cloud of dust, we moved toward the light in the next room.

"Oh no!" I cried out as I stepped into the next room and stared at my sister. She sat in a stiff-backed chair under a bright spotlight, a cone of white light.

Her head was down. Her red hair covered her face. She turned to face us, and I could see her eyes, wide with terror.

"Scarlet!" I screamed. "You're here!"

"Untie me!" she shrieked. "Hurry. Untie me!"

Her hands were tied to the chair behind her, and thick rope tied her ankles together at the floor.

"Riley—quick!" she cried. "Get me out of here!"

I dove toward her. I glimpsed Danitia close behind me. Carter and Cheng hung back.

"Is Mia here?" Carter shouted. "Have you seen Mia?"

I leaped into the cone of bright light. Scarlet twisted and squirmed, trying to loosen the heavy ropes that tied her down.

"Who did this?" I screamed as I grabbed at the ropes around her wrists. "Who brought you here?"

Before Scarlet could answer, I saw something moving across the room. Squinting through the bright light of the spotlight overhead, I saw shadow creatures dipping and circling.

I gasped. My hands drew back from the ropes. I heard Danitia cry out. Cheng and Carter backed against the concrete wall.

The shadows curled and bobbed in front of us, like a calm, dark ocean, waves low but readying to sweep onto shore. A tall wave of shadows, billowing across the room. Rising . . . rising like the tide coming in.

I couldn't move. I couldn't breathe. I'd seen these shadows in the video game, and they never brought good news.

"What's happening?" Scarlet cried. "Riley, untie me! Why are you just standing there?"

I didn't answer. I stood and gaped in horror as the shadows took shape. Three inky forms rose up from the billowing dark waves. In seconds, the shadows stood upright, became three separate figures.

I gasped as I recognized the faces of the three shadow people that faced us now. I knew two of them from the game. I knew their evil. And the third one I knew better than the others . . .

. . . Mia!

Mia encased in shadow, then stepping out of the dark covering into the light, her blond hair fluttering around her. Eyes wild with excitement. Her face a picture of total glee.

Mia. I never trusted her. From the moment I saw right through her skin in the sunlight . . . From the moment I saw a figure that looked just like her in the video game . . . Scarlet wanted to make her a friend. But I knew there was something wrong, something creepy about Mia.

And now she grinned at us, the shadows behind her. Her face glowed in the white light of the spotlight. And she pointed to the man and woman at her sides.

"These are my parents," she said. "I *told* you they would show up later. And here they are."

The man wore shiny armor over a purple robe. He was bearded and dark. His ears stood straight up, like wolf ears. And his snout of a nose and long-toothed grin made him look more like a monster than a man.

He *was* a monster. The Beast. I knew him well. I never defeated him in the game. I never came close. Mia's father was the Beast. And now here he was. And I let out a long breath because I knew we were doomed.

In the game, he stood like a man, but he growled like an animal. He tore people apart, ripped them in half with his teeth.

Margo, the woman—Mia's mother—was just as deadly. She looked frail and small, pretty and blond with a sweet smile—like Mia. But she had amazing powers of strength. She could grab your arm and snap it off. Or break your leg with one hand.

Whenever Margo and the Beast appeared in the *Shudder Mansion* game, I knew I was doomed. I never had the right weapons. I was helpless. They ended my game every single time.

And now here they were in real life. The smiles on their faces showed they knew they had already won.

What did they want?

"Let me go!" Scarlet cried. "Mia—tell them to untie me. Mia—please."

Mia ignored her. She turned to Danitia, Carter, Cheng, and me. "My parents asked me to make you all welcome," she said in her whispery voice. "Mom and Dad are so eager to meet you and to have you here."

"How did you do that trick of coming out of the shadows?" Carter demanded. "Are you magicians?"

He hadn't caught on. He had no idea what we were facing.

"Are you going to untie me?" Scarlet cried.

"SILENCE!" the Beast roared. "Silence—all of you. I make the game rules—not you."

"This is all a game?" Cheng asked.

"Yes, this is a game, and you have won," Margo said.

"*Escape from Shudder Mansion* is played all over the world," the Beast said, pumping out his chest as he bragged. "The most popular horror game of all time." His deep voice thundered off the basement walls.

"And now you have won, as Margo told you," the Beast continued. "Because you will all appear in the game sequel—*DEATH at Shudder Mansion.*"

30

The words sent a deep chill racing down my back. "You can't do that! You have to let us go!"

"You're crazy!" Carter shouted. "You have to let us out of here!"

"Let me go!" Scarlet begged, squirming in the chair, struggling with the ropes. "Please!"

Danitia had her hands pressed to her cheeks. Cheng stood behind her, arms crossed tightly in front of him, as if forming a shield. Mia stood between her parents, a thin smile on her face.

"Why are you young people unhappy?" Margo demanded. "You are all going to be *stars*!"

"Millions will see you die!" the Beast roared. "Millions! You'll be famous. Just think of it."

"We don't want to be famous," I said. I pointed to Scarlet. "Why have you tied my sister up? Let her go—*now*!"

"Your sister will not be set free," Margo said, taking a step toward me.

"The Beast is hungry," her husband said, stepping up beside her. He had his eyes on Scarlet. "The Beast must be fed!"

"The Beast must be fed!" Mia began the chant, and her mother joined in. "The Beast must be fed. The Beast must be fed!"

And as they chanted, the Beast began to change form. He dropped to all fours and grew and stretched. His body made horrible cracking sounds, and he opened his mouth, revealing rows of jagged animal teeth.

"The Beast must be fed! The Beast must be fed!"

Like a red-eyed panther, he growled from deep in his belly. Then he rose up over my sister, licking his teeth with a long red tongue and drooling . . . Gobs of yellow drool oozed onto Scarlet.

"The Beast must be fed! The Beast must be fed!"

"Riley—*do* something!" my sister shrieked in terror.

I knew I had only a few seconds before the Beast claimed his meal. But . . . what could I do?

Suddenly, I had an idea.

I had to get to the coal storage room next to the furnace at the back of the basement. I knew there was something there that might save us.

If I could get there, maybe . . . just maybe . . .

there would be a way to rescue Scarlet. And to keep all of us from having to die in this horrifying mansion.

But how could I get past the roaring, drooling Beast?

If I took off running, he would grab me in an instant. Then I would become his dinner instead of Scarlet. And I wouldn't be able to save any of us.

"Riley—hurry!"

Scarlet's shriek broke into my frantic thoughts. *How do I get past him? How do I get to the coal storage room?*

And then I spotted it.

My only hope.

31

I saw it on a small table against the wall to my right. It gleamed in the harsh light of the spotlight over my sister's chair. Squinting across the room, I realized what I was seeing.

A gold cup.

A gold trophy cup.

And I remembered it. I remembered it from the game I had played on the day Mia came to our house.

I remembered very clearly. I'd thought the gold cup was a prize. Playing the game, I'd moved to pick it up. And to my shock, it wasn't a prize at all. It was a trap.

The cup was filled with hundreds of angry spiders.

That was in the game. Now I was staring at the trophy cup in real life.

If I grab the cup ... If I pour the hungry spiders over the Beast's head ... Will I have a chance?

Will it distract him long enough for me to get to the coal room at the back?

I had no choice. I had to try it.

Without thinking about it any longer, I grabbed Carter with both hands—and I *shoved* him into Margo.

"Hey—!" She uttered a startled cry and stumbled to one side.

It gave me two seconds to move. I lurched across the room. Stretched out my hands—and grabbed the cup.

Yes! I had it in one hand!

The Beast tilted back his head in a deafening, angry roar.

I spun around—and dove quickly back across the room.

With a groan, I raised the gold cup over the Beast's head. Raised it high and tilted it over him.

I stood there with the gold cup tilted over the monster's head, not moving, not breathing, my entire body stiff with fear.

And watched as nothing poured out.

The cup was empty.

32

"Huh?" I let out a gasp. The cup trembled in my hand.

The Beast tossed back his head in a roar of triumph. His red eyes glowed. The drool glistened on his teeth.

He turned and began to lower his teeth to my sister's shoulder.

Scarlet screamed.

I raised the cup high—and smashed it over his head.

The Beast uttered a startled *whellllp*. And to my shock, the big creature flew apart. Burst into a million pieces. Just like that shadow I had seen that day on the back lawn.

I watched the pieces fly in all directions, like confetti blown by the wind. And then I was moving, faster than I had ever moved.

Margo and Mia stood in openmouthed shock as I darted past them. The light from the spotlight faded behind me and I ran into darkness.

I didn't care. I knew where I was going. I had to get there before Margo and Mia recovered and came after me.

Squinting into the blackness, I saw the enormous furnace, still and silent. And beside it, a wide doorway to another room.

The coal storage room. I could still smell the coal even though the room was empty. No one had stoked up this furnace in a hundred years.

If only I had brought a candle. Some way to see in this total darkness.

I knew where it was from playing the game. But how would I ever find it without seeing?

A tiny button. A tiny *reset* button.

I remembered it was on the near wall, somewhere near the bottom, almost to the floor.

I dropped to my knees. I frantically smoothed my hand over the bumpy stone wall.

If I could find the reset button . . . If I could push the reset button before anyone stopped me . . . Maybe this night would totally restart—just like in the video game.

Maybe we would find ourselves back outside. Maybe I could reset the whole night—and get us out of this terrifying mansion.

I heard footsteps. Running. Coming closer.

Shouts. Margo and Mia. Angry cries.

I spread my hand over the stones. I couldn't feel a button. I lowered both hands and moved them frantically over the hard bumps of the stone wall.

And yes . . . Yes! I found the button. Found it in the smooth molding near the floor.

I was shaking so hard, I couldn't keep my finger on it. I couldn't see. Couldn't think. Couldn't move.

But yes—I pushed the button.

Please work. Please reset the night. Just like resetting the game. Please. Please work.

Nothing happened.

33

I hunched there in the blackness, my finger still pressed on the button. Nothing moved. Nothing changed.

And then the darkness was suddenly replaced by a blinding flash of white. So bright, I let out a cry. I shut my eyes against it. But the pain of the sharp light came right through my eyelids.

Brighter . . . brighter. Finally, it faded. The pain lingered in my head. I waited for the light to be completely gone. Then I opened my eyes.

Whoa. I think it worked.

My dad pulled the car up to the curb. It was a dark, moonless night. Scarlet and I gazed up at Shudder Mansion, rising above the trees.

I can't believe we're going to spend the night in the old mansion, I thought.

"Don't forget the cooler," Mom said. "We brought a lot of drinks and snacks for everyone."

Behind us, a long SUV pulled up to the curb. Carter climbed out, followed by his housekeeper.

They moved to the back of the SUV and began pulling out all the electronic equipment Carter had promised to bring.

By eight o'clock, the whole team was gathered in the front entryway. We piled our jackets against one wall. Some of the parents began lighting candles and setting them up around us. Everyone was talking at once.

My dad began to clap his hands together and shouted, "Quiet, everyone. Can we have it quiet? We have a plan."

It took a little while for everyone to settle down. Mom and Dad both stepped into the center of the room. Their faces appeared to flicker in and out in the candlelight.

"We parents got together earlier this week and made a plan," Dad announced. "You guys are going to have a lot of fun tonight."

Fun? I thought. *Will it be FUN? I sure hope so.*

EPILOGUE

Hahahahaha!

Looks like Riley, Scarlet, and friends are going to live their terrifying night all over again. And again and again and again!

I think Riley pushed the wrong button. He pushed the RESET button. Maybe he should have pushed GAME OVER. Hahaha!

And why did all the parents run away screaming? Let's clear that up. It was their little joke. They planned it all along.

They didn't want the kids to get BORED. Hahaha.

Well, I bet they won't be bored now—since they'll be living the rest of their lives in Shudder Mansion!

I'll be back soon with some more shudders for you in another Goosebumps book.

Remember, this is *SlappyWorld*.

You only *scream* in it!

THE GHOST OF SLAPPY

Here's a sneak peek!

I stuffed a pair of woolly socks into my duffel bag and frowned at my sister Patti, who plopped on the edge of my bed. "Why are you staring at me? Why are you watching me pack?"

Her dark eyes flashed behind her glasses. "Because you're a hoot, Shep."

"Huh? I'm a hoot? What is a hoot? What are you talking about?"

She crawled over and began pawing through the bag. "Did you just pack a bar of soap?"

I slapped her hands away. "Get your paws off my stuff, Patti."

She stuck her round face into mine. "Did you? Did you just pack a bar of soap?"

"So what?" I said.

"It's an overnight in the woods, Shep. No one is going to take a shower."

I could feel my face grow a little hot. "Are you going to give me a break? I like to be prepared."

Truth is, I didn't really know *what* to pack. I'd never been on an overnight in the woods. I hate the woods. I hate the outdoors. And I'm not too crazy about the dark.

Why couldn't our sixth-grade class go on an overnight during the *day*?

Patti didn't back away. She sat beside my duffel bag with her arms crossed in front of her. I knew she was waiting to give me a hard time about something else.

Patti can be a pain. She is nine, three years younger than me. But she thinks she's the sensible one. Can she be bossy? Three guesses.

She has stringy black hair that she hates, a face as round as a pumpkin, and she has to wear glasses all the time. So do I. So do Mom and Dad.

Mom says it makes us look smart. But I think we look like a family of owls.

I tossed a flashlight into the bag. Patti pushed it deeper into the pile of stuff. "Could you go away?" I asked.

"Where should I go?"

"Brazil?" I continued to pack the duffel.

"You're a hoot, Shep," she repeated. "What did you just put in the bag? Was that bug spray?"

"Maybe," I said.

"It's almost November!" she shouted. "It's cold out. You're not going to need bug spray."

I pulled the can of bug spray out and tossed it on the bed. Sometimes Patti can be right.

Okay. So I was stressed. I wanted to bring all my blankets and my two soft pillows. I wanted to bring my sweaters and my sweatshirts in case it got really cold. But that seemed like too much.

Actually, I didn't want to bring anything. I didn't want to go. I kept thinking about being there in the dark with the trees rattling and shaking, and the wind howling, and all the wild animals lurking around everywhere.

And I knew I could not count on our teacher, Mr. Hanson, to help us feel safe. Hanson is a hor-ror freak. Some kids call him "Horrible Hanson" because he loves everything that's horrible.

He tells us horror stories in class and talks about all the old movie monsters as if they were real. My friend Carlos Jackson and I know that he's been saving up ghost stories to tell on the overnight. There's nothing Horrible Hanson would like better than making us all scream our heads off in fright.

Carlos likes ghost stories. But I have a real reason for *hating* them, a reason I can't tell Carlos.

I jammed two wool ski caps into the bag. It was getting very full.

Patti laughed. "You've packed everything you own. Is Tootsie in there? You'd better let me look." Tootsie is our cat.

Patti jumped to her feet and searched through my stuff again.

"If you're so into it, why don't you go in my place?" I said.

She shook her head. "I can't go on a sixth-grade trip. I can only go with the cool kids."

"Huh? Fourth-grade kids are cool? Are you *kidding* me? You only learned to tie your shoes last week!"

She stuck her chin out. "We don't tie our shoes. We're too cool to tie our shoes."

I stopped and took a step back. I didn't want this to turn into a fight. I needed Patti's help.

I pushed my glasses up on my nose. "Would you do me a favor?"

"I don't think so," she said. "What is it?"

"My sleeping bag is in the basement. Could you bring it up for me?"

She squinted at me. "No way."

"But, Patti—"

"Shep, you have to get over this basement thing," she said. "You have *got* to stop being afraid of the basement."

"I—I can't," I stammered. "I told you. That's where I always run into Annalee."

She tossed back her head. "Annalee. How did you ever make up a name like Annalee?"

I couldn't help myself. I started to shout. "I didn't make it up! It's real. Her name is Annalee."

She gave me a shove. "Oh, please. Give it a rest. Like I'm really going to believe that stupid ghost story." She raised her hands to shove me again, but I backed out of her reach.

"Annalee—" I started.

"There's no Annalee," Patti said. There's no ghost named Annalee haunting our house—and you know it. Why do you keep insisting?"

"Because it's true?" I said.

Patti rolled her eyes. "You're losing it."

"I don't know why she's haunting our house," I said. "And I don't know what she wants. B—but I know she's real. I saw her the day we moved in. And I've seen her again and again. And I have nightmares all the time about her."

"You dreamed her in a nightmare," Patti said. "She's not real."

"YES, SHE IS!" I screamed.

"Look at you. You're shaking," Patti said. She narrowed her eyes at me through her glasses. "You have *seriously* got to stop making up ghost stories. Ghosts do not exist, Shep. Everyone knows that ghosts don't exist."

I swallowed. "So you won't go down to the basement for me?"

She laughed. "You're a hoot."

I stopped at the top of the basement stairs. I peered down into the darkness. It smelled damp down there. It always smelled damp and kind of sour, like old newspapers or those dirty T-shirts that have been left on the floor in the back of my closet for a year or two.

I turned toward the kitchen. "Mom? Dad? Are you here? Can anyone go down to the basement for me?"

"Busy," I heard Mom call.

No answer from Dad.

I took a deep breath and reached to my neck for my lucky silver charm. Everyone should have a lucky silver charm. It has helped protect me in a lot of tough times.

It's actually a small silver bear head on a slender chain. You know. Like a charm on a charm bracelet. My grandfather Simon put it around my neck.

"Shepard, this is my lucky charm," he said. He was the only person in the world to call me by my full name. "I am giving it to you because my days are short and yours are long."

The cool silver tickled my skin.

"This lucky charm will never fail to bring you luck," Grandpa Simon said. "It has never failed me. You only need to press it between your fingers. Hold it tight and its luck will flow from the silver bear head to you."

I thanked him and adjusted the silver charm over my chest. Grandpa Simon died two weeks later. I've worn the lucky silver charm every day. I've never taken it off.

Now, I rubbed my fingers over it as I made my way down the basement steps. The stairs are wooden and steep, and they creak and groan like stairs in a horror movie.

As I neared the bottom, the stale aroma grew stronger. I heard the loud hum of the furnace against the back wall. I fumbled for the light switch.

Dim yellow light splashed over the basement. Two of the ceiling bulbs were out. But the one working bulb gave enough light to see the shelves against the far wall.

I knew my sleeping bag was rolled up on one of the shelves, next to my parents' skiing equipment and camping gear.

Holding my breath, I started to cross the basement. My sneakers thudded on the concrete floor. Dad was always talking about finishing the basement. Making it look nice. Turning it into a game room.

But somehow he never found the time to get it done. It still looked like a dark, damp, creep-out-time basement.

I kept my eyes straight ahead. I could see my sleeping bag tucked into a middle shelf. I was only a few feet away when a flash of light caught my eye and made me stop.

The light started out as a soft glimmer against the wall. Then it flickered like a tall candle flame and grew brighter. And as it did, I could see a figure forming in the center of the glow.

"Nooo . . ." A moan escaped my throat. "Annalee!"

She shimmered inside the flickering light. Just an outline of color. But then the outline filled in, and she stepped out of the white glow. A girl about my age. A girl in an old-fashioned, dark plaid skirt that brushed the floor. A high-collared white blouse with sleeves that billowed as if blown by the wind.

Her copper-colored hair fell below her shoulders and caught the glow of the light. Her eyes were large and blue and locked on me. She didn't blink. Her face . . . it was as pale as the light that surrounded her.

Hands reaching out to me, she appeared to float over the floor. The hem of her skirt made no sound as it brushed against the concrete.

As she loomed closer, I took a step back. And cleared my throat to shout: "Go away, Annalee!" My voice trembling and shrill, ringing off the low basement ceiling and the heavy walls.

"Go away, Annalee! You don't exist!"

A strange smile spread over her pale face. Too sad to be a smile. Her red hair fluttered around her shoulders. Her eyes stayed locked on mine.

My hand fumbled for the silver bear charm under my shirt. I grabbed it and squeezed it. "G-go away!" I stammered.

But she slid forward silently.

"What do you *want*?" I didn't recognize my shrill voice. "Annalee—what do you *want*?"

Her lips moved. Her words were lost, just a whisper of air.

She raised a pale, slender hand. Reached out— *to grab me?*

"Noooo!" I uttered a frightened cry—and toppled backward. I fell over a low pile of cardboard boxes. The boxes crashed to the floor. I thrashed the air with both hands as if grabbing for the ceiling.

But I fell hard. Thudded onto my back on top of a hard box.

"OOOOF." The air whooshed out of my chest. I struggled to catch my breath.

Annalee floated over me. Her hair flew around her face. Her lips moved again. Again, I couldn't hear what she was saying.

Her hands were curled into tight fists. She waved them at me.

Threatening me?

My heart pounded so hard, my chest ached. I couldn't think straight.

And then a voice from across the basement broke through my panic: "What *was* that? Shep? What fell?"

My mom, shouting from upstairs.

I squirmed and twisted, struggling to climb back onto my feet.

Mom's running footsteps thundered on the wooden basement stairs.

And before I could stand up, she was there. Leaning over me. Hands pressed to her waist. Her expression startled and confused.

"What on earth—"

I forced myself to sit up. "I—I—I—" I sputtered.

"Did you fall?" Mom asked.

"It was the GHOST!" I cried.

Where was she? I glanced around the basement, but I didn't see her.

"The ghost, Mom. Really. I—"

Mom offered me a hand and helped pull me to my feet.

"Annalee. She's here, Mom," I cried. "She's here."

Mom's mouth dropped open. She started to say something to me—but stopped. I realized she wasn't looking at me. Mom was squinting into the darkness.

"Oh, wow," Mom murmured. "I see her."

I gasped.

Mom took a few steps toward the center of the room. "There you are," she said, pointing. "I see you. You *do* exist, after all, don't you. Come into the light, Annalee. Do you want to come upstairs?"

About the Author

R.L. Stine's books are read all over the world. So far, his books have sold more than 300 million copies, making him one of the most popular children's authors in history. Besides Goosebumps, R.L. Stine has written the teen series Fear Street and the funny series Rotten School, as well as the Mostly Ghostly series, The Nightmare Room series, and the two-book thriller *Dangerous Girls*. R.L. Stine lives in New York with his wife, Jane, and Minnie, his King Charles spaniel. You can learn more about him at www.RLStine.com.

The Original Bone-Chilling Series